THE
Thirteenth
FAIRY

A Never After Tale

THE
Thirteenth
FAIRY

A **Never After** Tale

Melissa De La Cruz

MACMILLAN CHILDREN'S BOOKS

First published 2020 by Roaring Brook Press, a division of
Holtzbrinck Publishing Holdings Limited Partnership

Published 2020 by Macmillan Children's Books
an imprint of Pan Macmillan
The Smithson, 6 Briset Street, London EC1M 5NR
Associated companies throughout the world
www.panmacmillan.com

ISBN 978-1-5290-2275-9

1 3 5 7 9 8 6 4 2

Book design by Elizabeth H. Clark

A CIP catalogue record for this book is available from the British Library.

Printed and bound by CPI Group (UK) Ltd, Croydon CR0 4YY

For all the magic in my life
For my ever-after family
Mike & Mattie always
For my friends who believed
Jen Besser
Richard Abate

Contents

Prologue

The Unvitation

O nce upon a time in the days of old, eleven fairies gathered at court before a child to hold. Only eleven, for the twelfth was dead and the thirteenth was missing. An invitation for every fairy – except the thirteenth – had previously been sealed, sent and delivered: a formal request to come forth and bless the sweet newborn princess.

Now all of Never After had come to Westphalia to celebrate this long-awaited day. Creatures old and new, of every height and hue – from towering dragons, their armoured scales glittering gold and green, to warty goblins and rambunctious dwarves. There were garden gnomes seated on toadstools and tiny pixies fluttering their dragonfly wings, slender forest sprites and weathered crones. There were merchants and farmhands, milkmaids and pageboys. There were grand dukes and great ladies, and too many onlookers to count. For a collective breath had been held in the kingdom for countless nights, countless souls wishing upon countless stars for the overall health of every perfect petite finger and toe. It was time to exhale.

A new princess! The precious future of the kingdom.

On the day of the christening, handsome King Vladimir and beautiful Queen Olga sat atop their thrones, gleaming smiles upon their lips, brilliant white teeth shining and blinding. A dazzling display of both pride and prize as they hosted a fete of impressive size.

It was almost like magic, as if, with a snap of the fingers, it had happened at long last. *Voilà*: a baby. All that once was, was now forgotten. A fresh new present, dreamy and vast, devoid of the unfortunate past.

And yet. And yet.

There was a motive behind each mirror.

What was that? A maniacal laugh sounded in the distance if you listened closely enough. But none could hear it, because none *would* hear it.

The babe – Princess Eliana – had been longed for; that

she was desperately wanted was the understatement of the century. The king and queen had been in the throes of despair, hoping and waiting for this baby girl. She was the stuff of dreams delivered.

Princess Eliana was safe and warm, swaddled in cotton and fluff, wishes and moondust. She'd received a kind glance from every assembled guest, and each passing moment was its own tiny and fleeting miracle. Delight flitted through the air, leaving sparkles of joy and wonder in its wake. It was universal bliss to leave a kiss upon the little darling's fingertips.

But something was amiss. Something, *yes, something indeed*, was peculiar. None could pinpoint it, or examine it in depth. No one wanted to look through the thinly laced veil, a superb glamour to distract and divert.

Instead! Let us feast on the plates of pastries and pies provided for all. Blueberry, raspberry, lemon sorbet, rich layered cake. Wine and spirit, drink and dance. Let us gaze at the elaborate ball gowns, jewels and crowns.

For this was an open invitation, come one, come all.

Come all . . . except one.

The members of the court chattered among themselves, trading rumour and speculation, whispered into various pointy and curious ears. Questions laced with a hint of dread and agitation.

'Where is Carabosse?'

'Where is the thirteenth fairy?'

'What of her blessing?'

The court murmured and muttered, fretted and frazzled. Carabosse, the thirteenth and most powerful fairy in all of Never After, was nowhere to be found.

No invitation had been sent.

Quite the opposite.

An *un*-vitation, if you will:

The princess has finally arrived.

The king and queen celebrate their child.

However, your presence is not required.

It is unwanted, unwelcome, and undesired.

STAY AWAY, CARABOSSE.

Harps and flutes played melodies of lullabies for the royal babe with rosy cheeks and bright copper eyes. She yawned and stretched, then wailed. And cried. And cried some more. She wanted her mother.

Her mother!

Where was her mother?

Was she not there, on the throne? Holding a goblet to her lips, oblivious to the cries of her sweet daughter?

No!

4

That was not her mother.

No!

That woman on the throne – that was not her mother. The mother she would never know was not there.

Her mother was dead.

The late queen Rosanna would never hold her daughter, the newborn in the forefront of the court, the centre of this new world that kept spinning without her.

For Queen Rosanna was dead.

That woman on the throne, married to her father – that woman was not her mother.

Was it only a few weeks since King Vladimir had knelt at Queen Rosanna's graveside and wept? It could not be, but it was. A few weeks. Mayhap a few days. Not enough time for proper mourning, no room for sufficient grieving. A king had lost his queen, yet no dirges were sung, no banners lowered in memoriam. No respect paid for his previous wife. No tears, no years of wait. Not even a single moment of reflection. Not even a *what if* remaining on his tongue.

No eulogy made, the soil still fresh on the grave, King Vladimir remarried. As if he'd inhaled at her passing and exhaled a new life.

There he was, sitting proudly with his new wife, Queen

Olga, and their cherub – the already-famous princess Eliana.

But largely unmentioned in the tales to come is that the thirteenth fairy, the uninvited fairy, the fairy Carabosse, was the late queen Rosanna's sister and hence Princess Eliana's aunt.

Carabosse had warned Rosanna about the mortal world, warned her about leaving the safety of the forest. But Rosanna didn't listen. Rosanna gave up her magic to follow her heart, and now she was dead and buried underground.

But Carabosse was very much alive.

And, at last, she had arrived.

Un-vitation and all.

A fevered hush swept over the court as Carabosse strolled in, gown trailing behind her. The tales told after this day speak of an ugly crone, hunchbacked and withered, of a threatening and vile fairy enchantress. A wicked witch, wreathed in black, with eyes like braziers and a voice of snakes and sandpaper.

The tales are wrong. The tales are twisted and untrue.

For Carabosse was breathtaking.

Tall and dark and wild and striking. She had Rosanna's long black locks and scissor-cut cheekbones, her petal-pink lips and regal bearing, but Carabosse's eyes were all her own. Rosanna's eyes were chestnut brown, as warm as rain. Carabosse's eyes were as black as night and as deep as the ocean's depths. Her dress was gossamer and ebony, dipped in gold and sparkling with the light of a thousand fireflies. Her bare feet scarcely touched the floor. She did not walk but glided over the ballroom with hardly a sound.

The music stopped. The creatures froze. Worry reverberated and bounced off the castle walls. An eerie quiet unsettled the merry hall. More whispers sprang from lips. Gluttonous gulps became silent sips. And then came the pointing from various fingertips. All aimed at Carabosse.

'At last! She is here!'

'What will she do?'

'What has she come for?'

She eyed her sisters, the assembled fairies all in a row, with sorrow, and many hung their heads in shame. Carabosse, the eldest and best of them, strode purposefully to her niece's crib, a wooden sleigh covered in twine and vine, and lifted her beloved sister's baby in her arms. This little girl was all she had left of her dear Rosanna. Her heart nearly burst at the sight of the child. The resemblance, uncanny, almost as though she were looking into her sister's own warm brown eyes.

As she whispered to the babe under her breath, then bent her head to kiss her stolen niece, whom another woman claimed as her own, their first moment together was also stolen – by a shrill shriek.

Queen Olga looked askance. 'What are you doing? Hand me back my child!' she cried.

'Your child,' Carabosse echoed, with a slow rise of a perfectly arched eyebrow as she turned to the new queen. '*Your* child . . .'

'My child,' said Queen Olga, with eyes like braziers and a voice of snakes and sandpaper.

'I have come to bestow my blessing,' said Carabosse.

And the court held its breath . . .

Part One

Wherein . . .

Filomena Jefferson-Cho embarks on an unexpected adventure.

Jack the Giant Stalker arrives on the scene to pull her into Never After.

Our heroes are attacked and escape in the nick of time.

Part One

Chapter One

The Girl

Filomena Jefferson-Cho walks along the pavement, looking down and wondering if there are more cracks in the kerb than terrible things that happened to her today. Because in her small, sleepy and perpetually sunny hometown of North Pasadena, California, where nothing ever happens, she's quickly learning that anything that can go wrong . . . *will*.

At least for her.

School *sucked*. She'd left her laptop at home, which triggered an automatic demerit; the cafeteria was out of the 'good' chocolate milk; and she got a C-minus on her

Algebra One Honours quiz. And even though she's the only sixth-grader in eighth-grade algebra, which is an honour in itself, it still stung.

Worst of all, her best friend, Maggie Martin, is currently ignoring her to hang out with the Fettucine Alfredos – the obnoxious rich kids who order fancy pasta delivered from the snooty restaurant across the street. Unlike the rest of the class, who line up for hot lunch or eat the same old vegan bologna sandwich, like Filomena does every day.

But there were a few bright spots in her day, for which Filomena is grateful. One, her neurotic and *way* too overprotective parents finally allowed her to walk somewhere alone for once. Two, the thirteenth and final book in the Never After series was released today.

Oh, joy! Oh, profound happiness! A new book! And not just a book, but the *finale* to the series! All the questions answered! The princess rescued! The villains vanquished! The hero's journey victorious at last!

It's the best thing to have happened since the *last* book in the series came out. Maybe the best thing to have happened even since the latest smartphone was released. The one with the better camera and the talking cartoon emoji. Or was that *two* new smartphones ago? Who can keep track?

Filomena can't contain her excitement, especially as she's allowed to go and pick it up all by herself. Her parents never let her walk anywhere alone, and she's twelve years old, for British Kit Kats' sake. Yeah, British Kit Kats. They're smaller and yet . . . somehow *more* chocolaty. She prefers them to the bigger and infinitely less tasty American version. Most things that are bigger are not necessarily better, she has discovered.

But back to the point: her oversheleteredness. It's reached the point of suffocation. She can hardly breathe most days! She deserves some freedom, a little trust here and there. A playdate or two, maybe? To ride a bike or scooter without a helmet or an irrational and overwhelming fear of bad guys lurking nearby, just waiting to snatch her up?

For as long as Filomena can remember, her parents have been talking about all kinds of abductions, even legends about fairies who steal kids, switching them for one of their own. Her parents have very vivid imaginations. (They're writers. It comes with the territory.)

Filomena's parents treat her like a precious treasure, a cherished gift. Little do they know that most people actually avoid her. Or bully her. Or make fun of her. At least, people her age do. Everyone else just seems generally uninterested in her. Come to think of it, maybe it would be better if she were snatched by fairies.

Maybe fairies would be nicer than most kids. Maybe if they were half goat and half human, or had glowing green skin and horns, they wouldn't tease her for being smart, wouldn't ask her where she came from (here) or rudely wonder if she was black or Asian or white or what on earth was she (all of the above). For the record, she has curly dark hair, dark brown eyes and skin the colour of maple syrup. Maybe fairies wouldn't think she was weird for reading so much; instead, they'd pick her brain about it – literally. Oh, wait, that's aliens, not fairies, and maybe that would be bad . . .

Either way, it doesn't matter to her parents. The bottom line is that Filomena is *never* allowed to walk home from school by herself. Or go anywhere by herself, for that matter. They made it crystal clear that this afternoon would be the one and only exception, because they know how important the Never After books are to her. And, since both her mom and dad had looming deadlines, they weren't able to give her a ride to the bookstore.

Still, regardless of their smothering and overly protective ways, Filomena loves her parents. She also loves her Pomeranian puppy, Adelina Jefferson-Cho. And her beta goldfish, Serafina Jefferson-Cho.

14

She named them that way so that they would all sound like they belong in the same family. The way some families give all their kids names that rhyme (Stan, Jan, Fran) or names that all start with the same letter (Carrie, Corey, Caitlyn). It screams, 'Hey! We're a family unit, in case you couldn't tell by our appearances!'

Because people sure can't tell by the Jefferson-Chos' appearances. Filomena is adopted. Her dad is Korean-Filipino and her mom is British. No one in her family looks like the others. And, despite her parents' compassion and kindness and deep abiding love, she often wonders if they have any idea how she feels. How not knowing who your biological kin are or what they look like can plague you. How wondering why you were given up can haunt you, making you feel sort of un-special from the start. No matter how special her parents did make her feel.

So, yeah, 'family' means a lot more to her than it might mean to the average twelve-year-old. It means *almost* as much as the doe-eyed singer who just left the world's hottest boy band to start a solo career. Riley Raymond probably means just as much to the vast majority of other girls her age, and even to an immeasurable number of boys her age. The boys just might not admit it yet because kids can be so evil. They poke and poke and poke at anything they can find that's different about you.

Filomena hates that about humans as much as she adores Riley Raymond's floppy brown hair and falsetto singing voice.

What else does she adore? Many things. Well, she doesn't love any one thing, animal, parent or pop-star heartthrob in any particular order. However, what she might love the absolute most (don't tell her parents) are the books in the Never After series.

And the thirteenth and final book is out today.

THE THIRTEENTH AND FINAL BOOK IS OUT TODAY! (*Use megaphone here.*)

But she's cool. She's not *running* to the bookstore.

Nah, she's cool as a cucumber. Walking. Backpack slung over her shoulder. And it doesn't have princesses on it, either, OK? She's not a child. Not any more. Not like her parents consider her, anyway.

Her backpack is sleek, stylish. It's black with grey straps, and instead of a princess, or a cute animal with extra-large eyes, or a fancy designer logo, it has the sigil of Never After on it – a gold circle around a tree with a heart carved on its trunk. Inside the backpack are Never After-themed pencils and a Never After pencil case. Proving devotion to the fandom through merchandise is one of her favourite hobbies. If she could get a Never After tattoo, she would, but she's too young, and her mother forbade it.

She can nearly smell the bookstore from here. It's maybe another fifty steps away. She's got everything she needs.

The money to buy the book? *Check.*

The blaringly loud whistle her mother gave her before she left for school this morning, just in case she needed a way to alert others that she was in danger on the walk home? *Check.*

Her favourite Never After bookmark, just waiting to be placed in the new book she's about to buy? *Check.*

A huge grin on her face that she's trying to stifle but unfortunately cannot, because she's too excited for words? *CHECK.*

After the day she's had, this book is pretty much her prize simply for surviving the last eight hours.

Because her luck is about to change. She is only five steps away from the bookstore – two if she leaps – and her heart starts pounding louder the closer she gets to the door.

She's almost there. And soon she will be reading the climax, the ending, the finale of the series of books that defined – nay, *divined* – her childhood.

She can hardly wait to find out what happens next!

Chapter Two

The Book

Alas, what happens next is not what anyone expected. Sad trombone.

Filomena reaches for the door handle like she's reaching for her dreams and accidentally whips it open a little too excitedly.

She feels a familiar blush warm her cheeks and she shrugs, apologizing as she walks in. 'Whoopsie,' she says, and offers a nervous laugh. 'Sorry about that. I think the wind took it and—'

'It's quite all right, dear,' the bookseller at the desk says with an understanding smile that is also full of pity – a reaction Filomena's not unused to.

Filomena smiles back and fidgets with her hands as her eyes scan the bookstore for what she's expecting to find: a huge, freshly filled stand full of copies of the new Never After book. A ladder of books. A *tower* of books. A ziggurat! A pyramid! An explosion! Just like there was for all twelve books before this one.

The Never After series is one of the most popular book series of all time. In the twelve preceding volumes, readers followed the adventures of Jack the Giant Stalker and his lovable, loyal crew of ragtag friends as they met heroes and heroines of popular fairy tales and battled to keep the land of Never After safe from a slew of evil witches, villains and ogres. In the twelfth volume, Jack and his company were running for their lives, hounded to the edge of a cliff and certain to fall to their deaths. Would he find yet another ingenious way to escape and defeat his enemies once and for all? She certainly hopes so. The book ended on a literal cliffhanger.

Filomena is itching to read the thirteenth book. She has waited so long. A whole year!

But, instead of the books, she finds a group of fellow die-hard Never After fans – better known as Nevies – standing around, grumbling, seeming as disappointed and let-down as she's starting to feel. They look like they're about to take out pitchforks and riot. Then she hears someone say, 'Ugh! No way! It can't be true! No book?!'

Filomena's heart starts to sink. Another feeling she's grown used to.

Since she's there alone and isn't the most, er, socially outgoing individual, she approaches the familiar and friendly face at the counter instead of the crowd. Mrs Stewart is not just a bookseller – she's also a former novelist who opened a bookstore after she'd sold gazillions of copies of her one book and decided she wanted to devote her life to reading instead of writing. Mrs Stewart is also not just a bookseller but one of Filomena's few friends.

'Excuse me? Mrs S?' Filomena asks. 'Do you have the new Never After novel in stock? It was supposed to come out today, and I figured—'

'Oh, honey,' Mrs Stewart says, her sympathetic smile growing more sympathetic. 'We figured too. We were all ready with our fairy-dust cookies and our stalker hats.' Indeed, many of the Nevies gathered at the store are eating crumbly sugar cookies and wearing the pointy green hats that Jack famously sports in the books.

Filomena's heart sinks past her stomach to the floor.

'Except apparently it isn't being published, after all.

Not this season. Not ever. The author's long gone, and there's no book.'

'The author – you mean – Cassiopeia Valle Croix? She's dead?' gasps Filomena.

'Dead or disappeared – they won't say.'

Filomena's mouth drops open. 'So . . . wh-what do you mean? The book won't be published? But it's been advertised all year. And the cover's on the website. How can that be?'

'It just is.' Another sad head shake.

'It won't be published? At all? Never?'

'Never ever, that's what they say,' says Mrs Stewart, frowning. 'Apparently, Cassiopeia wrote all twelve books at once, years and years ago, and her estate has been publishing them all this time. But she never wrote the thirteenth one. Her estate thought they would find it in her files, and promised the publisher they would send it when they did. The publisher kept saying it was coming, hoping the estate would find it. But at last they all had to come clean. There is no thirteenth book. Not anywhere. Either it wasn't written, or it's lost, but, in any case, it's not being published. I'm sorry, honey.'

Filomena is so devastated she cannot speak. Her mind reels with disappointment. She wants to shake a fist at the sky and scream, 'Noooooo!' But instead she just turns pale.

'What can I tell you?' Mrs Stewart sighs again. 'Sometimes life is stranger than fiction. This is one of those times. We definitely don't have the book in the store. But I don't know, maybe try online?'

(They don't have it online. They don't have it anywhere. The book does not exist. This is something Filomena confirms later that evening after much browser searching.)

Filomena opens her mouth to protest – to protest what, she isn't even sure – but stops herself. 'Never?' is all she asks.

'Never,' Mrs Stewart echoes sadly.

Feeling just incredibly, ridiculously, completely disappointed and discouraged, Filomena takes one last look at the dejected crowd of Nevies and heads back towards the door. *Maybe we should riot*, she thinks. *Maybe we should throw some books around, kick a few journals. Something. This will just not do!*

She leaves the bookstore in a huff. All she has left is a long walk home after a terrible day.

She's too busy feeling sorry for herself to notice that someone started following her about thirty paces ago.

But when she does finally sense a presence behind her

– a very *unwanted* presence – she feels an uncomfortable paranoia start to wiggle its way into her bones. She tries to shake it off, convincing herself it's only her parents' neuroses playing tricks on her.

But when she turns and spots the person behind her, a tall figure draped in black, her eyes widen. She spins back round, pretending she hasn't noticed him.

Oh no, she thinks. *Is he a kidnapper? Just like they always warned?*

She reminds herself that her emergency whistle is tucked inside her backpack. She tugs the bag closer to her in preparation, hoping she'll be fast enough to get away if this person really is a Filomena-snatcher.

Her parents have made her suspicious of everyone. She tries to shake off the fear again, convincing herself she's just overthinking things.

But a part of her can hear every scary story her parents have told her, about missing kids and mysterious disappearances and changelings left on doorsteps while the real children are whisked off to fairyland, and she wonders if their morbid prophecies are about to come true. Maybe fairies really *are* coming for her. Maybe she's never going to see her parents again, ever. Maybe this is the end of her.

Her heart rate picks up again. Only now it's not due to excitement. It's the exact opposite of excitement.

What would that be?

Oh. That's right.

That would be fear.

Chapter Three

The Boy

Filomena squeezes her eyes shut for a nanosecond and then blinks rapidly, staring straight ahead. This cannot be happening, she tells herself. Surely there is not a random person lurking behind her, about to kidnap her. But when she quickly turns a corner, the person does too, and when she slows down to look at the window of an ice-cream store, she can see him linger in front of a florist just a block behind.

Yep, some freaky rando is definitely following her.

Serial killers or wicked criminals or evil fairies do not exist in her world, at least not in safe, sleepy, sunny North

Pasadena, where nothing ever happens. Or . . . she thought they didn't. They're not supposed to, anyway.

But what if they did? What if something actually happened here in North Pasadena? Something awful and dangerous?

If something did, she would fight. Yes, never surrender. That was a theme in many books. And she has read many a book. Both her parents are writers – hence the lively imaginations. Words are part of her world.

And *escaping* her world is one of her favourite pastimes. (Though she'd never tell her parents that.)

Oh no. Her parents! They'll go absolutely nuts if she isn't home by dark!

But I'm not allowed to be kidnapped! she'd tell her kidnapper. *My parents will be very mad at me if I'm kidnapped!*

Her parents! The fear of their wrath and the desire to avoid another three-hour lecture on how to stay safe in an emergency (if she failed to avoid one altogether) is enough to keep her going. Plus, she has her puppy and beta goldfish to survive for. If she's abducted by fairies or taken by a nefarious child-grabber, who will take care of those two?

As she tries to convince herself not to look back,

reasoning that this person is just a figment of her imagination, she can't help it. She turns round again in what she hopes is not an obviously frantic motion, to see if that someone is still there.

Oh! Yes, he is, and he is *definitely* following her.

She walks faster and looks down to watch her sneakers steadily padding the pavement. One foot after the other. Left, right, left, right. Distracting herself with this steady march, she focuses on her shoelaces. The frayed white edges. The double knots, a safety precaution.

But she can still hear his feet trailing her own. An unbroken beat, too close, that echoes her own footsteps. It sounds as if he's mirroring her pace, her movements. The joint steps create a strangely hypnotic rhythm.

She knows she needs to stay calm; her parents lecture her about this sort of thing all the time. But she has never had to intentionally *try* to stay calm, except when her parents are freaking out and she gets sucked into the hysteria. Unlike several other unpleasant things, like finding a humiliating post on social media or a nasty note left in her locker, sheer terror is definitely *not* one of the things she's used to. But she's feeling it now.

She knows he's still behind her. And he's getting closer.

She looks back again, probably in a more obvious way

now. When she turns her head, her eyes accidentally meet his. Gah!

Filomena takes mental notes of details to remember about him in case she needs to provide a description to a police sketch artist. Hair colour: to be determined (covered by hood). Eye colour: grey? Height: tallish. Shoe of choice: . . . Wait, are those *clogs*?

She glances behind her again to get a better look.

Weird thing number one – besides the fact that he's *following her* – is that the boy is wearing a *cloak*, not a hoodie as she'd first assumed. Weird thing number two, she notices that the part of his arm that is exposed is covered in vines – just like Jack Stalker's in the Never After books. Weird thing number three is that this somehow comforts her and settles her galloping pulse.

Suddenly she feels silly. She shakes her head and almost laughs aloud. He must be a fellow Nevie! She breathes a sigh of relief, and instantly the panicked internal screams stop.

She slows her steps to a normal pace. Perhaps even a leisurely one, to allow him to fully catch up to her. Maybe he saw her at the bookstore, where he, too, was waiting for the thirteenth book, only to sadly discover that no one knows when or *if* it is ever going to come out. (Never. It is never coming out.)

Filomena excitedly turns to him as he gets close, his footsteps almost next to hers. 'Can you believe it's not being published? I was *so* looking forward to the end—'

But, instead of commiserating, the boy suddenly pushes her to the ground.

'Hey!' Filomena yells in annoyance, about to give him a piece of her mind, when a powerful force crashes down on the pavement inches from where she's standing.

What the—? Where did that come from? What is happening?

Instinctively, she shields her head. She's read enough books to know she has to protect herself.

Am I under attack?

She frantically tries to reach for her backpack to find her whistle! Oh man, her parents are going to totally freak out if this makes the news.

But there's no time to panic as another thunderbolt hits the pavement with a deafening boom, the brightness crashing against the concrete path right in front of her.

Then evil, cackling laughter fills the air.

Wait! What was that? Did I imagine it, or were we just hit with an Ogre's Wrath?

Ogres aren't real, though! They're just in books! Never After books, to be clear. And they certainly can't walk right off the page and into your hometown to try to scorch you.

'Get up! We've got to run!' says the boy. 'She's followed us here!'

Who's followed whom here? Filomena wants to ask, but she's too shocked to do anything, not even stand. For a second or two, she wonders if this is some sort of joke. If perhaps it's just an expensive, elaborate spectacle put on by the publisher or author to give superfans an interactive experience.

But when a third thunderbolt crashes right next to them, almost singeing her backpack, and the cackles screech into madness, the joke suddenly isn't very funny. Smoke lingers in the air beside her, and there's a black mark on the ground where the bolt just struck.

She instantly reaches for her hair to see if that's where the scorched smell is coming from, but she's stopped by the hand of the stranger she has almost forgotten about in all this bizarre chaos.

'Come with me if you want to live!' the hooded boy says, offering his hand.

She stares at him in disbelief and confusion. The cackling grows increasingly louder around her, the shrill laughter ricocheting off the booms of the thunder, creating a terrifying rumble and high-pitched screech.

Just like that, her panicked internal screams start again. Filomena takes his hand. She wants to live.

Chapter Four

The Series

Hand in hand, they run from the thunderbolts. There's no time to consider the potential risk or wonder where he's taking her. All she knows in this moment is that she has to run. Even if that means running off with a stranger. Sorry, Mum!

More thunderbolts strike the ground around them, but they duck and weave, luckily avoiding being hit. A bolt crashes between them, separating the two from each other. But when the smoke clears, Filomena finds the boy frantically waving at her.

'This way!' he yells, heading towards a half-hidden

alley.

She follows him, running as fast as her last-person-picked-for-the-team legs will allow her. He takes a sharp right, and she almost trips over nothing other than her own fear.

They continue to run as more thunderbolts shoot from the sky, and it feels as if the strikes are tracking their steps through the deserted alley. The cackling gets louder and louder, bouncing off the brick walls of the buildings on either side of them.

Things look dire, and despite the sheer adrenalin and her rapid heartbeat, Filomena decides she has to do *something*. If this is an Ogre's Wrath – and it certainly sounds and smells and scorches like one – there might be a way to stop it. And if this boy in front of her, who is guiding her through the pandemonium, is a fellow Nevie, he won't think what she's about to say is all that weird. Maybe he'll even know the words.

As her feet pound the pavement with each step and her breathing becomes heavier, she goes over the spell in her mind a few times. Fumbling over the words will only lead to failure.

Filomena reaches out to the boy and tugs on his cloak, signalling him to slow down. 'Repeat after me!' she yells.

'What? Now is no time for talking!' he replies curtly.

She glares at him in response, yanking his arm to force him to stop. Because if there's a tiny chance she may be right, then *he*'s wrong.

Quickly, she takes hold of both his hands, knowing that their combined energy will do better than hers alone. She practises the fairy spell in her head, envisioning the words she's read so many times.

Then: 'Ogre, ogre, cloaked in clover, I cease your wrath, three times over! Go back to the bog where you belong, go back to Orgdale and don't be long!' she chants, and after a brief moment, he follows her lead, adding his voice to hers.

Just as quickly as it started, the attack stops. The thunder quiets, disappearing in the distance of her memory. The cackling softens until it fades completely.

'How did you know that would make it go away?' the boy asks, a look of wonder in his eyes.

'Because a fairy spell stops an Ogre's Wrath, just like in the books, duh!' she replies. 'And sends the ogre back home.'

'What books?' he asks.

Filomena wants to talk about why and how – and *whoa!* – they were just attacked by an Ogre's Wrath in

North Pasadena, where nothing ever happens, but there's genuine confusion on his face, so it appears she will have to put aside her own confusion temporarily.

Oh well. So much for thinking he was a fellow Nevie.

She shrugs out of her backpack and removes a book from inside. 'This book, of course!'

It's a massive golden tome with a treasure chest on the front and a vine pattern tracing all around. The twelfth and penultimate book in the series.

He stares at it. 'Where did you get that? It's a spellbook.'

Filomena rolls her eyes and wonders whether she should humour him. Is this a test? Is he trying to quiz her on her knowledge of the series? Little does he know she's read all the books front to back, countless times over, not just favourite scenes but the *entire* series. At this point, she could nearly repeat the stories word for word, as if she'd written them herself.

Yeah, she's not buying it, his playing-dumb demeanour in this deserted alley after they were *just* attacked with magical thunderbolts and heard the laughter of the ogre queen that every fan knows about.

Um, could they talk about that? What happened just a minute ago?

But he's still staring at the book with a concerned look

on his face, so it looks like they'll have to talk about the series. Which is fine! Filomena loves talking about the books.

'You're telling me you've seriously never read this?' she asks him as she hands him the book, doubt lacing her tone as her eyes trace the vine round his arm. The one that matches the vine on the cover of the book she's showing him. He certainly *looks* like a Nevie.

'Read it?' he repeats, like it's a mystery to him, as he flips through the pages.

She shakes her head and offers an irritated sigh. But she explains that the book is part of a very popular fantasy series, adventure books based on fairy tales.

'Fairy tales?' asks the boy as if he's never heard the words.

'Yeah, it's about a bunch of kids and their adventures with princesses and frogs and witches and stuff like the lightning strike that just tried to kill us . . . *here*. I mean, what was that? Some kind of promotion, do you think?'

'Promotion?'

'Why do you keep repeating what I'm saying?' Filomena demands.

'I'm just trying to understand what you're talking about,' the boy says, crossing his arms.

'That makes two of us. I mean, doesn't it even bother you that we could be ogre toast right now if I didn't know the spell? By the way, that really happened, right? I'm not dreaming? This is real?'

'Of course it happened,' he says, as if she's not making any sense.

'But it can't be! Ogres aren't real.'

'Of course they are.'

'In books, yeah,' she responds. 'But fiction and reality differ.'

'Fiction?' he repeats.

'Stop doing that!' she says, getting fed up. 'You're acting like you have no idea what I'm talking about!'

'You're absolutely right. I don't. Beg your pardon for not introducing myself sooner. I'm Jack the Giant Stalker. Jack Stalker for short,' he says, taking a bow.

She laughs in response. 'Oh, the same name as the dashing hero of the series. Classic. Nice try.' She snatches her book back. 'And you've never read the books. Right,' she says under her breath.

'Dashing?' he says under his, with a quirk of a smile.

'Huh?' she asks.

'Nothing.'

She is about to walk away, but he stops her once more.

'Wait,' he tries, reaching for the book again. 'May I?'

With a disgruntled huff, she hands it over to him. 'If you stop being weird, yeah.'

'What did you call this again?' he asks, studying the book.

'A fantasy book,' she says.

He laughs now, but it's disbelieving. A shake of his head, and then, 'These books aren't fantasy. The world of Never After is real. As real as those scorch marks over there.'

Filomena looks to where he's pointing, at the blackened ruins in the middle of an otherwise perfectly ordinary pavement. She literally cannot believe her eyes. 'But everyone knows they're just stories!' she wails.

'Just stories?' he says, thumbing through the pages. He doesn't look up at her as he continues to scan the book. 'This looks like a history of the fairy tribes. If you've read this, then you know about the war we've been fighting for years against the witch of Orgdale and her legions of villains and henchmen. How they've relentlessly attacked us, from poisoning princesses to cursing mermaids. And how her army of ogres has been invading our lands as well.'

He says it so casually, so nonchalantly and with such

conviction that she wonders if he's insane. But that doesn't stop her from responding. If it's a test of some sort, she's not going to waver.

'Of course I know about the war between the fairies and the ogres,' Filomena says. 'That's the whole point of the book series. To see if good wins over evil in the end.'

'But it's not just a book,' Jack insists. 'It's real.'

OK, so first he's never heard of the Never After books and now he's telling her they're real? This is getting annoying. She grabs for the book again and takes it from him. 'Just quit it. It isn't funny any more.'

'I'm not trying to be humorous,' he replies seriously.

'Just go away, please. The thunder and cackling were impressive, really great trick. And your cosplay is excellent. Obviously, you're actually way too into the books, and it's kind of creepy.' She finishes stuffing the book into her backpack, where it's safe and sound, and zips the pack closed.

'Please, hold on,' the boy says, looking at her intently. 'One moment.'

She snaps her head towards him, giving him an irritated scowl. 'Leave me alone! I'm going home now. Don't follow me again or I'll call the police. I have a whistle!'

She shifts the backpack so it's comfortably resting on her shoulders. She gives him one last hard stare so he knows she means business.

'I wasn't following you!' he says.

'Yes you were!'

'OK, I was! But I saw you had the Golden Oak on your pack, and so I thought maybe you were going back to the Heart Tree, and I was lost, and I figured I could just follow you there.'

'Heart Tree? You mean the portal that connects all the lands of Never After to each other?' she asks, eyes narrowed.

'Well, yes. So you *do* know where it is!'

'Um, no, because it doesn't exist! It's just in the books! And this is *merchandise*,' she says, pointing to the sigil on her bag. 'Stuff they sell to fans once they've read the books but still have money to burn!'

'The books?' asks Jack.

'The books!' It takes everything Filomena has in her not to stamp her feet.

'Let's please not have this argument about what's real and what's not again,' he begs.

'We're not going to. But stop following me.'

'Fine.' He rolls his eyes.

'Fine.' She rolls hers.

She eyes him suspiciously and turns away, holding tight to her backpack straps as she starts running again. Only this time, she's not running for her life but running away from the cloaked boy who just helped *save* her from the latest disaster of the day.

Once again she watches her sneakers pad the pavement. Only now, she's counting down the moments until she's back on the street – the same place she just desperately fled from.

She almost laughs at the irony, and she probably would if she weren't so out of breath. Usually she tries to avoid the whole miserable species, but right now she's never wished harder in her whole life than to be surrounded by people.

Chapter Five

The Friend

Jack watches the girl walk (well, run) away. The frown on his face is apparent, and he considers her obsession with the vine on his arm, wishing he could let it spring out and wrap her up and bring her back to him. But, judging by her tone, she probably wouldn't like that at all.

If only she would help him. He has to get back home; who knows what's happening there. He stumbled into this world by accident, and now he has to stumble out of it somehow. Why did the portal take him *here*, of all places? He's heard that the land of mortals is strange and dangerous, but he didn't count on the natives being so *unfriendly*.

Zera warned him once that they don't believe in Never After over here, but he didn't realize it was *true*. Then again, how did that girl know a fairy spell? And what was that book she was carrying?

'Hey!' Jack calls out again. He realizes he doesn't even know her name. Although she knows his. And what did she call him? The dashing hero of the story. Yeah, he'll take it.

He waits for a moment, hoping she'll turn and come back. But she's long gone. Her long legs have taken her away.

He shakes his head and starts making his way to the end of the alley, considering his next move.

A sudden rustle in the bushes startles him, followed by the pop of a head out of the centre. 'Great job, chap. Seems like you really won her over.'

Jack clutches his chest and tries not to scream. 'You scared the living beast out of me, Alistair! Little warning next time?'

The short, ruddy-cheeked boy finishes climbing out of the bushes with an innocent yet amused smile. He plucks some green leaves and twigs from his rough-spun tunic and close-cropped dark hair. 'Sorry. Didn't want her to see me. She seemed spooked enough. Well, can't blame her.

Ogre's Wrath and all. I nearly tinkled me trousers meself. You'd think I'd be used to it by now.' He shudders, then kicks his boots against the building to get the last of the dirt from himself.

Jack offers a sympathetic smile and pats his friend on the shoulder as he finishes dusting himself off. 'It's hard to get used to.'

Alistair removes one of his boots and inspects the bottom of it. Then he makes a face like he's going to hurl, and brings the boot closer to Jack. 'What do you think this is? I can't get it off. It's pink and . . . stretchy and things are stuck in it.'

Jack pushes the boot away and says, 'That's quite all right. Keep your sticky things to yourself, please.'

Alistair shrugs and puts his boot back on, then stomps a few times for good measure, trying to get the pink goo off.

Jack watches his pal and smirks, stifling the impending laugh bubbling up in his throat.

Alistair is one of Jack's greatest friends, despite how different they are. Alistair is a head shorter than Jack, with a sweet, open face, and endlessly loyal. His good nature tends to get him into troubling situations, but his sense of humour and positive attitude tend to lead him out of them.

'What's cosplay?' Jack asks Alistair as they continue walking together.

'Beats me,' says Alistair. 'What did you want with her, anyway?'

'She carried the mark of the Golden Oak, I thought she could help us find our way back to the tree. Plus she had a spellbook and knew how to deflect an Ogre's Wrath.'

'But she told you to go away.'

'I noticed,' says Jack.

'What do we do now?'

Jack sighs. 'Let's get something to eat. We'll try to find the Heart Tree again tomorrow. We need to let Zera know I got you out of Parsa in the nick of time.'

'I can't believe they raided that entire kingdom for one lamp,' says Alistair.

'Well, they didn't get it this time, and they never will,' Jack says. 'Not if we can help it.'

'Queen Olga knows we're here for sure, though, sending her wrath through the portal and all. She's never going to give up on that lamp,' says Alistair.

'If she returns, we'll be ready for her,' says Jack. 'But she'll never get it. The only way to the lamp is through us.'

Alistair shudders, then quickly changes the subject. 'Anyway, I read this guidebook Master Carl once wrote about the mortal world. I think we need to hunt something called cheeseburgers. That doesn't seem too hard. I don't think they can run very fast.'

'Cheeseburgers?' Jack repeats.

'The guidebook mentioned how they can hide in a system in your body for years, especially if you get them from a palace called the Golden Arches. But the guide also says they are not rare. In fact, they are very common here.'

Jack nods, taking in this information.

Alistair continues. 'According to my map, there's a place called Inside-And-Out Burger not too far from here. However, it does not mention how we get inside.' He gasps, accidentally crinkling the map. 'Oh heavens, what if we go in and can't get out? You know I've never been good at riddles!'

'Let me see that,' Jack says, taking the map from Alistair's hands. 'If mortals can do it, surely it can't be that hard.'

Chapter Six

The Family

After what feels like a lifetime, Filomena sees her house come into view. Home is a sleek, three-storey white and grey contemporary-style house with a two-car garage. The driveway wraps round in a circle, and she always walks the full length at least once before going inside, for luck.

It's a pretty neighbourhood of tidy pavements and green lawns. She wishes her parents would let her walk her puppy, Adelina Jefferson-Cho, on her own, but instead they hire people to do the dog-walking for them. No one in her house enjoys being outside very much.

As she approaches the front door, snagging her house

key from the key ring in her side back pocket, she looks around to make sure the boy who *dared* call himself Jack Stalker – her literal stalker now – isn't still following her. Out of the corner of her eye, she notices a movement in the trees by the park across the street, but she dismisses it. Probably just a squirrel.

Breathing easier when she sees she's alone, she unlocks the multiple locks and walks inside, entering the code on the pad by the front door so the system knows the house is safe and she's not a stranger breaking and entering.

Adelina runs up to Filomena, circling her feet, always the first to greet her. Filomena picks the puppy up in her arms and kisses her until Adelina is crying and trying to get down. Filomena supposes there *is* such a thing as too much love, and she should know.

She plops the dog down, then looks up at the security camera closest to the door and stretches her mouth wide with her fingers, giving it a silly face.

She wasn't kidding when she said her parents were paranoid. They have not one but five deadbolts on the front and back doors, as well as various alarms and security cameras everywhere. Some are hidden throughout the house, in every crevice, every nook, every spot a criminal may not think to look. According to Filomena's parents, they can never be too careful.

It wasn't until Filomena was old enough to go to an assortment of birthday parties thrown for an assortment of spoilt or indifferent kids that she noticed not everyone lives like her family does. One lock on the door and a security system, sure, but no one ever uses it. People leave their gates unlocked, their windows open. After all, everyone in her small town does like to proclaim that 'nothing ever happens in North Pasadena'.

Well, that is definitely not true. Not after today, anyway.

Filomena is still unconvinced it wasn't a huge marketing launch, although she can't deny the blackened ruin of a pavement. But it's absurd! Things from books stay in books. There has to be a logical explanation for what happened, and she's sure if she doesn't dwell on it, it will soon come to mind. And, if not, she will just stop thinking about it.

She debates whether she should tell her parents about what happened today. If she does, they will never let her go anywhere by herself ever again. They'll probably also think that her brain's been curdled by reading too many Never After books.

Except since both her parents are writers, they don't find her fascination with the series strange at all. In fact, they encourage it. They love that she reads. It keeps her safe in the house ninety-nine per cent of the time.

The sound of hurried footsteps on the attic stairs notifies Filomena that her mother is home. Bettina Jefferson tramples down, harried, hair in a messy bun, talking about deadlines. Filomena's mother is always talking about deadlines. Deadlines and kidnapping are her favourite topics of conversation.

Her cell phone is pressed to her ear, and with the other hand she pushes away the stray strands of hair that have escaped the bun and covered her forehead. 'Of course I'll have the first draft to you by Friday! Why ever would I not?' She bites her lip and rolls her eyes. 'Darling, of course I know how important this is.' An impatient nod that the person on the other end of the phone can't hear or see. 'I understand the concept of publishing, yeah? When have I ever not delivered? Right, except for that time . . . and that time . . . right, and that. Well, they can *try* to take back the advance, except I've already spent it all, yeah?'

As soon as she catches sight of Filomena, her eyes widen and she waves. Filomena smiles in response and mouths, *Hi, Mum.*

Her mother is still saying, 'Uh-huh, uh-huh,' as she mouths to Filomena in between, *Where's the book?*

Filomena holds out her empty hands and shakes her head.

'Bobby darling, Filly's here, so I've got to run. Don't stress. I've just got to the wedding chapters and I'll send it to you in a wink. Cheers.' She clicks the button to end the call, and Filomena follows her into the kitchen, where Mum tosses her phone on to the counter. 'I should've put the blasted thing on silent so my agent can't harass me any more.'

Filomena laughs and sits on the closest stool at the island, its surface a granite slab in cream and grey, like the other countertops. The kitchen is open and bright, with streams of sunlight peeking in through the blinds.

A freshly delivered paper bag on the counter by the fridge holds tonight's dinner. Her stomach starts to grumble at the sight of it, the aroma reminding her how hungry she is.

Her mum *always* orders delivery or takeout. She calls it *takeaway*, one of her Briticisms. Filomena's family never goes out to eat – strangers, hello – and her mum can't cook a single thing to save her life.

Filomena occasionally feels guilty about making fun

of the bullies at school and dubbing them the Fettucine Alfredos for ordering in lunch, when her own parents order in so much.

'What's for dinner?' Filomena asks.

'I've got a lovely chicken parm from that new restaurant that just opened. Smells divine, doesn't it? I'm starved. I've been writing all day, trying to finish this book.' Her mum reaches into the cabinets to grab plates. 'I'm so behind. As usual. The pages from yesterday were trash. I put them in the bin.'

'You'll get it done, Mum. You always do.'

'Thanks, darling,' her mum says, setting the plates at the table and giving Filomena a quick kiss on the cheek. She hugs her daughter tightly. 'So how'd it go at the bookshop? I was worried sick about you. I've been watching the thingy that tracks your movements all day, just in case something happened.'

Filomena briefly wonders how accurate the device is, whether her mother saw her stray from the path and rush into the alley, and if she should tell her what happened: the thunderbolts, the sound of maniacal laughter, the strange boy . . . But her mother writes contemporary romance fiction, not middle-grade fantasy. Unless the boy turned out to be a secret billionaire who would whisk Filomena away to an exotic island, Mum wouldn't get it. Filomena isn't allowed to read her mother's books yet, which is why she's very knowledgeable about them. Especially because her classmates bully her by nastily demanding to know whether she's read certain pages. Page 157 of Mum's latest book is exceptionally saucy.

So Filomena shrugs and says, 'Everything went fine. I'm fine, Mum. See? No kidnapping today. I'm still here, in the flesh.'

Her dad comes up from the basement and enters the kitchen, giving Filomena a kiss on the forehead. Filomena beams. She's her dad's favourite kid. Of course, she's his only kid – that's why she's the favourite.

'Did you get your book?' Carter Cho asks, taking off his glasses and wiping them with the hem of his wrinkled T-shirt. He's handsome and trim, neat and tidy in his grey sweater and trousers, in contrast to Mum's messiness.

'Ugh, no,' Filomena says, staring blankly in front of her. 'The book's not available. It wasn't even published.'

Her parents look at each other for a moment and then turn their confused faces on their daughter.

'Not published?' asks her mom.

'That's odd,' says her dad, frowning.

'Mrs Stewart said all the bookstores were told it's never

53

going to be published. Turns out the author's been dead for ages and supposedly didn't leave the thirteenth book. Maybe she never even wrote it.'

'Oh no, honey,' her mum says. 'I'm so sorry. You were really looking forward to this.'

'I know,' Filomena says, sighing. 'Maybe the estate will find it one day but until then, no one knows when or if it will ever come out.'

'That's strange,' her father says. 'Typically, traditional publishing is pretty strict and dead set when it comes to release dates.'

'Yeah, tell me about it,' her mum chimes in. 'Bob's a maniac about my deadline. How am I supposed to write twenty thousand words by Friday?'

Dad chuckles. 'You'll get it done, sweetheart. You always wait until the last minute and then whip up something fantastic and heart-warming that brings your hero and heroine together in a spectacularly romantic ending!'

Filomena's father writes mysteries featuring a very fastidious detective given to cheerful proclamations. He thinks there's always a resolution to every story. Meanwhile, every romantic lead in Mum's story resembles Dad. Even the secret billionaires have a penchant for Korean food.

He turns to Filomena and snaps his fingers, his eyes shining. 'I got an idea,' he says. 'I know this won't replace the excitement you felt for the release of that book, but how about we play a little Never Ever?'

It's a popular game based on the Never After book series. As much as she loves it, her father's right. Nothing can replace the book she spent a year looking forward to reading. But she offers him a forced smile anyway, grateful for his attempt to cheer her up, and she goes along with it.

'Fine! But I'm the princess,' says Filomena.

She always plays the heroine.

Chapter Seven

The Pasta Posse

The next day, Dad drives her to school as usual. 'Still upset about the book not coming out?' he asks when he notices her looking glum on the back seat.

'You could say that,' she tells him.

He reaches behind to pat her leg and then looks ahead at the road. They drive the rest of the way in silence, her father unsure how to comfort her about the book, Filomena unsure how to tell her dad what's really on her mind.

She doesn't know how to say that it's not just the book that's troubling her, but how much she dreads going to school every day. That the bullying has got out of hand lately. That she can't walk to her classes without being harassed by the mean, popular kids. That she doesn't feel as if she can be herself there, or be there at all without being bothered or made fun of in some fashion. She doesn't know how she can ever tell him that these kids are ruining her life – without breaking *his* heart in the process.

Her parents care about her so much – maybe *too* much, if that's possible. Knowing that she's hurting would only hurt them, so she doesn't want to share her sadness with them. This isn't their fault, or their fight. Plus, if they tried to intervene, it might just make things worse. If the other kids knew she had snitched on them, the teasing would just worsen. Nothing good happens for anyone who tattles. That's a fact. Snitches get stitches. Middle school and prison code: sort of the same thing.

Filomena's father joins the long car-park line staffed by teachers and administrators with megaphones to direct the traffic at their fancy private school. The worst thing about being bullied at Argyle Prep is that her parents are actually paying for her to have the privilege of attending the school. Dad plants a soft kiss on her cheek and tells her to have a good day.

'Love you, Fil,' he says just as the troll-faced principal opens the car door for her.

'Good morning, Filomena! Mr Cho!' Principal Nightingale booms with forced cheerfulness as she holds the door open. At private schools, principals also act as the morning valets, as part of the school's we're-all-in-this-together facade.

Dad gives the principal a tight smile. At PTA meetings, Mum and Dad are very vocal about their displeasure in the way the school is run, and the principal, who once declared there is no such thing as bullying in the school ('So what do you call it, then?' asked Dad), is no one's favourite.

Filomena smiles at her dad despite the tension she feels and says, 'Love you too,' as she reluctantly scoots out of the car. 'Bye, Daddy.'

Filomena at school is very different from Filomena at home. For one, as she walks closer to the entrance, her body shrinks and folds into itself, almost as if she were losing height, confidence, space. She's trying to make herself invisible. Trying to make herself disappear in front of her peers.She checks her phone and sees that she has just enough time to make it to her locker and get to class before the second bell. If all goes smoothly, at least, which it usually doesn't.

She scans her outfit again. It's a free-dress day, otherwise known as dress-anxiety day. Filomena is much more comfortable in the school uniform. She surveys her clothing, examining it for anything strange or unusual that someone could tease her about. Her sneakers are normal enough, on trend, even. She's stopped wearing her favourite purple combat boots. Apparently, they weren't up to par with what the other kids considered *normal* to house your feet in.

Her jeans fit all right, not too tight, not too loose. Her black faux-leather jacket should at least help make her appear tough, especially with the ripped T-shirt underneath. But she doesn't feel that way inside any more. Not since they've beaten her down – literally and figuratively – for so long.

Alas, the Linguini Losers are right there when she walks through the school doors. They're waiting in the hallway near her locker, as has become the daily norm.

There's nothing special about them. The head girl isn't even particularly pretty or funny or smart – just aggressive, with a bossy air and a threatening attitude. But she does have seven short, bland, generic kids who dumbly follow what she says.

Troll army, thinks Filomena, just like in the Never

After books. Except all the mean girls at her school are named after flowers – Posy, Daisy, Petunia, Carnation – while the mean boys are all named after sports teams – Tex, Angelo, Lake, Buck. They would be intimidating except that the boys are even *shorter* than the girls. (It's middle school, after all.)

Filomena makes her way to her locker. As she inches closer, the Rigatoni Ralphs jump in front, blocking her.

'Come on, the bell's going to ring,' says Filomena meekly, even though she towers over them.

'Too bad,' sneers Posy, her hand across the locker. 'I heard you did well on the science test the other day.'

What science test? wonders Filomena, and then she remembers. *Oh, the one everyone else failed.* Posy and the noodles had posted their horrific grades – 52 per cent, 65 per cent, 48 per cent – on their social media accounts, joking and laughing with one another, and so Filomena had done the same, thinking she was innocently joining a meme. Except her score – 102 per cent (because she got everything right, including the extra-credit question) – was apparently nothing to laugh about.

'You think you're smarter than us, huh?' Posy demanded.

'Um . . .' Filomena wants to tell them about the C-minus she got in Algebra One Honours, except it would only make them hate her more. She's already two math levels ahead of the rest of her grade.

The other kids giggle, taking part in taunting her. One of them snatches for her backpack, pulling it away from her so that she stumbles a little.

Another grabs at her hair as she tries to regain her footing, knocking her off balance yet again and yanking her backwards.

'Dumb move,' her assailant chimes in, sounding disgusted while gripping her hair hard and pulling.

Filomena flinches, reaching for her hair – which took hours to flatten. It's another thing her peers take delight in teasing her about, accusing her of being neither here nor there in her heritage and looks.

'If you're so smart, do you even know if you're black or white or yellow?' someone else taunts.

This is getting so old. She's heard all the jeers before.

'Yeah. Your own parents didn't want you. You think your teachers do?' another kid says to her, a statement that still stings her every time.

Filomena turns red. She tries to fight back the tears threatening to spill. If she's late for class again, she'll get a suspension, and she doesn't want to tell the teachers about the bullying. She just wants it to go away.

If only there were a way to make it stop. The rude and snide remarks. The pushing. The snickering. The teasing. The things that are slowly chipping away at her confidence – little by little, day by day, until one day she'll just disintegrate into nothing.

But she knows she needs to try to find the strength to fight back. Wallowing, retreating, flinching – that only makes things worse. It feeds them, eggs them on. Backing down just infuriates the bullies more.

She reaches for her locker, but Posy slaps her hand away.

'For a smart kid you're pretty stupid,' she hisses.

'Yeah, and Filomena's an ugly name too,' someone else cackles.

Now all the kids are surrounding her and slapping her. As usual, there are no teachers or administrators around. All the teachers are in their classrooms and the staff are in their offices. No one ever sees anything, which is why the principal says there's no bullying in the school. It looks playful, but it's not. The slaps hurt, almost as much as the words. Filomena can't take it any more. Not even for a second longer. Her name isn't ugly! It's ancient Greek and Arabic. It means 'strength' and 'courage', and it also means 'friend'. Above all, her mother told her, it means 'beloved'. *You are loved. We wanted you so much, baby.*

Filomena tries to dodge the blows, but they keep landing, even as she twists away from the others, their insults ringing in her ears. *Ugly. Stupid. Know-it-all. Show-off. Loser. Unwanted.*

She needs to make it stop! If it would only stop! Then she hears a voice in her head: *Never After is real.* Immediately a spell comes to mind, and she speaks it out loud: 'Time and tide await none but me! Stop the clocks until I order thee!'

And, just like that, the ruckus stops.

She opens her eyes.

Everyone is frozen.

The kids standing all around her are paralysed mid-insult, mid-hit, their faces ugly and contorted.

Never After is real. That's what the boy said yesterday. The boy who called himself Jack Stalker. And speak of the devil . . . The voice in her head isn't just in her head at all.

'Good work!' says Jack, who's suddenly appeared, almost as if she's conjured him there. But now he has a friend by his side.

'Alistair?' says Filomena.

'Yes!' says Alistair happily. 'She knows who I am!' He turns to look at Jack with a pleased grin on his face,

63

moving his eyebrows to showcase his smugness.

Of course Filomena knows who he is – it's Alistair from the books, Jack Stalker's loyal friend. This new boy is dressed in the same dun-coloured robes Alistair wears in the Never After series, and he has a treasure chest tattooed on his cheek. But . . . he's different from what's on the page.

'You're much cuter than I expected,' she tells him. 'And you don't have an odd accent at all! I mean, it's a little Cockney, right? But that's all.'

Alistair is a bit miffed. 'Well, gee, thanks. I'm from Parsa, but I went to boarding school in Albion. It's a pleasure to meet you too.'

'My mother's from Brighton,' says Filomena, who knows Albion is a kingdom in Never After that closely resembles England. 'And you don't look like a goblin at all! The writer really took some liberties with your description,' she informs him.

'Goblin?' sputters Alistair. 'I'll have the writer know that I'm a prince!' he declares.

'Are you now?' says Filomena.

'One hundred per cent,' says Alistair with a smile, and it's almost like she can *hear* the glint shine off his white teeth. 'Anyway, you know our names, but we don't know yours.'

For a moment Filomena hesitates, her inner alarm

sounding a *stranger danger!* warning. But, then again, they *did* just help her get away from her enemies. And what was that saying? *The enemy of my enemy is my friend?*

'Filomena Jefferson-Cho,' says Filomena, greeting both boys.

'Alistair Bartholomew Barnaby,' says Alistair. 'You already know that's Jack.'

'I do,' says Filomena, because if this is Alistair, then that's *really* the famous Jack Stalker standing next to him. And that really was an Ogre's Wrath she deflected yesterday. Which means . . .

'Wait.' She shakes her head. 'Did I just cast a time spell?' she asks. She looks back at the Frozen Lasagnes (get it?), hoping they never thaw out.

'Yes, you did, which means we don't have much time,' said Jack, looking at his pocket watch.

'Right,' says Filomena.

Time has stopped only until she does what she has to do, which is get away from the petulant Pasta Posse.

'Let's go!' says Jack.

'Wait!' Filomena reaches into her locker and grabs her stuff. She needs her books!

Books in hand and Filomena away with a head start, time unfreezes, and the slimy noodles begin to move again.

Chapter Eight

The Trees

When time starts up again, the Fettucine Alfredos are standing in front of Filomena's locker, but Filomena is no longer there, where she should be, according to logic and, well, general rules of time and space. All that's left of her is the scent of peachy body wash and coconut shampoo, and in her place stands a whirlwind of confusion.

Posy and the noodles stare at one another in disbelief, quizzical looks on their faces.

'Where did she go?' Posy snaps. 'She was literally just here!'

'That little snake!' another kid chimes in, kicking Filomena's locker.

Filomena is, they notice suddenly, running down the hall shoving her books into her backpack. And she now has two oddly dressed kids with her. Kids the noodles don't recognize. They've never seen the pair around school, and they basically know everyone – by taunt or by haunt.

'Who are those weirdos?' one of them asks.

'Who cares! How'd she get there so fast, anyway?' another replies.

'Beats me. She was *just* here a second ago . . .'

'Quit wasting time!' Posy barks at them. 'She's getting away!'

Filomena makes a mental note never to post her test scores on social media again, no matter how much fun it seems to be. It's just not worth it!

The Alfredos give chase, tailing Filomena and the two boys.

Filomena finds herself out of breath yet again, wondering why each time Jack Stalker shows up she is forced to run for her life. She supposes in the books he is always doing the same (running, adventuring, hopscotching over fiery pits and whatnot).

And, just like in the books, he's kind of cute.

Not that she noticed.

And how did he magically show up here anyway, right after I cast that spell? She continues to run as fast as she can, following Jack for a second time, automatically trusting him. After all, she's read twelve books about him; she knows him like he's practically her best friend. Plus, Alistair is here. Everyone loves Alistair. He's a fan favourite. He's the kid who basically carried Jack up Mount Gloom so that he could destroy the Ring of Infinity before that horrid ogre queen could get her hands on it.

Has she lost her mind?

What if Jack and Alistair are just figments of her imagination? But they seem so *real*.

Jack's cloak is flapping in the wind, with Alistair trundling as fast as he can behind. Filomena turns to check whether the Alfredo gang is still following them. They are. In fact, they've closed the distance a little too much for her liking. Beads of sweat form on her forehead as she races towards the school exit, and she momentarily wonders how Alistair is making out with all this cardio. He has the shortest legs of the three of them, and if she's feeling it she knows he and Jack must be too.

'Get back here, you little witch!' Posy yells after Filomena.

Filomena turns round to see her pursuers quickly catching up. They're only a couple of metres behind!

Why do popular people always have to be so athletic?

She tries not to let their impressive speed discourage her as she trails Jack and Alistair. The exit doors are just ahead. If they can make it outside, maybe the Alfredos will give up and let them go, so that the Spaghetti Squad themselves don't get in trouble for being late for class. Although it's probably inevitable now that they'll get tardy marks.

To her dismay, as she, Jack and Alistair blow through the front doors to the outside, the Alfredos are still close behind them, ramming through the same doors seconds later. The doors didn't even have a chance to close!

Oh God, oh God, oh God, Filomena repeats in her head, trying to keep herself calm despite the impending doom heading straight for her. She knows she'll be dead meat if they catch her – and that is not a metaphor.

'You can run, but you can't hide!' one of the Alfredos yells.

'Wait till we get our hands on you!' another troll warns.

'Awful clichés – is that the best they can do?' says Alistair.

'They don't have a lot of imagination,' says Filomena,

grinning even as she looks back, sweating under her layers.

She, Jack and Alistair are outnumbered. There are too many of the Rotten Rigatonis. They're an arm's length away now. In a second, a pasta pile-on will commence, with Filomena at the bottom of it.

She nearly screams out of sheer fear of what's to come, when suddenly she smacks head first into Jack, who's stopped running and has turned round with his hands outstretched before him, a ferocious look on his face.

'Move to the side!' he bellows.

Filomena is confused for a split second. Then she realizes what he's about to do: the vines from his arms are already slipping out, ready to lasso and attack his enemies.

'Woo! Let it rip!' cheers Alistair.

'Jack, no!' she cries. 'You can't hurt the Alfredos!'

'What! Why not?' he yells back, still holding his arms out, his vines tingling with tension, ready to spring.

'You just can't!' she begs.

As much as she wants him to, as much as she would love to give them a taste of their own medicine and relish revenge, she knows he can't. Jack Stalker is magic, and he can't waste it on these lousy noodles. It would be like a bear stomping on an ant.

At last Jack relents and, instead of attacking, practically flies from the pavement, and leaps for the tree closest to the schoolyard, with Filomena and Alistair close behind.

'Up here!' Jack says, scrambling through the branches like a squirrel. It's almost as if the tree were letting him climb it, leaning down and lifting him up.

Filomena and Alistair follow, and the branches practically zoom them all the way to the top of the tree, tossing them higher and higher.

'Whoa!' Filomena says, almost slipping off a limb. But a vine wraps round her wrist and tugs her up, and she sees Jack ahead, the vines wrapped round his wrist too, as he helps her up.

He grins at her.

(OK, he really is way too cute.)

When the action stops and the three of them are safely nestled in the highest point of the tree, which no one could comfortably climb without some sort of assistance (like, ahem, *magic*), they sit still. Filomena checks her body over to see if she feels any broken bones, injuries or even scrapes, but there's no pain. No sign of any kind of wound. She looks down.

The Alfredos are left on the ground. They're stomping their feet and screaming profanities, waving their hands in the air, fists balled up in a threatening manner. Filomena can't make out everything they're saying; she's laughing too hard.

'Whoa!' she says. 'That was so cool! It was just like in the seventh book when the oak tree gently guides Jack and his friends up to safety at the treetop!'

'I speak the language of the trees. I just asked for a little assistance,' Jack says with a modest shrug. 'Yesterday I tried to tell you it's not just a book. Do you believe me now?'

Does she have a choice? Yesterday she was almost killed by a cackling thunderbolt. Today she stopped time and escaped from her enemies with the benevolence of a sentient tree. Now she's sitting on said tree with two of her favourite fictional characters who look very, very real. She can see the sweat beads on Alistair's forehead and the vines beginning to retract round Jack's arms.

She looks at them thoughtfully.

They look back at her patiently.

'Yeah, I guess I do,' Filomena tells them.

'Good, because we need your help,' says Jack, relieved.

'We sure do,' adds Alistair.

'OK,' says Filomena. 'But first tell me how you got here.'

Chapter Nine

The Hunt

Jack situates himself on the branches to make it more comfortable. He's breathing a little heavily; running away from an adversary was the last thing he wanted to do. He was ready to unleash the vines on those . . . those . . . what did she call them? *Alfredos?* Did they all have the same name?

Alistair steps gingerly on to the branches to manoeuvre closer to Jack. 'How much should we tell her?' he whispers loudly.

'Why?' asks Jack.

'What if she faints or falls out of the tree?'

'Ahem,' says Filomena. 'Guys? I'm right here. I can hear everything you're saying.'

Alistair gives her a thumbs-up. 'No worries, dear. I read something in the guidebook about mortal hearts and how faint they are, so I'm just being careful.'

'My heart is not faint, thank you very much. Didn't you see how much running I just did? I don't even do cardio regularly, and I was fine,' Filomena points out.

'Cardio?' Alistair asks.

'It's like, um, exercise. Running. Spinning. That sort of thing, to get your heart rate up.'

'Spinning? Like a top?' Alistair asks, curious.

'No, like on a bicycle. Do you have those in Never After?'

Based on their confused looks, it appears they don't. She shrugs.

'So I take it you don't run regularly, then?' says Alistair.

'Not if I can help it.'

'Why not?' Jack wants to know.

But Alistair is on her side. 'Why would anyone run unless they had something to run from?' he says reasonably.

'Well, people here do it to stay in shape,' she explains.

'Like a circle? Or a square?' asks Alistair.

'No, in shape, like . . . well, like him,' says Filomena,

jerking her thumb at Jack, the fittest of the three.

Alistair shakes his head in confusion. 'Mortals,' he says under his breath.

'Mortals? Aren't you mortals?' Filomena says. 'I mean, you both look human. Aren't we the same?'

Alistair looks insulted. 'We're Never Afters. You're not.'

'He doesn't mean to offend,' says Jack. 'And we're human . . . but—'

'But you're from fairy tales, so you're not real,' says Filomena, beginning to catch on.

'That word again,' says Jack with a grimace.

'I mean . . . I guess you're not like us. In the book it says fairy tales are timeless . . . which I guess makes you immortal?' she asks.

'Quite,' says Alistair. 'We never grow old, but we can perish. There are rules about it, though. Complicated ones. Thankfully, our demise hasn't been something we've come close to experiencing. Yet.'

'We haven't answered your question,' says Jack thoughtfully. 'You asked how we got here in the first place. Well, you know about the Heart Tree portal. That's how.'

'Right. But, also, how'd you get here? To school I mean. How'd you know where I'd be?'

'We've been following you,' Jack admits. 'I know

you told me not to, but, well . . .'

'And we couldn't find any cheeseburgers to hunt,' Alistair adds.

Filomena tries not to laugh. Hunting cheeseburgers?

'Anyway, we're not supposed to be here at all. We just ended up here when we were trying to get away, and this is where the portal took us,' Jack says.

'Get away from what? Or whom?'

'Queen Olga, of course,' says Alistair. 'Duh.'

'Right,' says Filomena, who never likes to say the ogre queen's name out loud for fear of bad luck.

'In the books, does it mention that she's looking for something to secure her power and keep all the kingdoms of Never After under her spell?' Jack asks.

'Yeah, but we never find out exactly what it is. She thinks it's the Ring of Infinity or a Seeing Eye or the Magic Mirror, but it's none of those things,' Filomena tells them.

'No,' says Alistair sadly.

'In the stories, you are always able to grab the object or destroy it before she gets it, anyway,' says Filomena.

'Well, yes,' says Jack, attempting modesty. 'So far.'

'So what is it? What is she looking for now?'

'Aladdin's lamp. The genie of the lamp has powerful

magic that Queen Olga wants for herself.'

'But I thought the lamp has been kept in a secret place since Aladdin's wedding,' says Filomena.

'It's supposed to be,' says Jack, exchanging a glance with Alistair. 'But that was a long while ago, and in the meantime she's been searching everywhere in Never After for it for centuries. If she finds it, then we're . . . what did you call it? Ogre toast.'

Filomena pales considerably.

'Don't worry,' says Alistair. 'Jack will make sure that doesn't happen—'

'Because you're Jack Stalker, and you never shy from adventure!' says Filomena, quoting from the enthusiastic words on the back of the books.

'Right ho!' cheers Alistair.

Jack shrugs and looks a little shy. 'Well . . . I guess.' He regards Filomena keenly. 'You know, you should come with us to Never After. You seem to know a lot about our stories. You could be helpful.'

'Except my parents won't let me go more than several hundred feet away from my yard, let alone travel to another world.' Filomena shrugs.

'Really?' says Alistair. 'My parents let me go any-where.'

Jack slaps his head. 'You don't have parents. You're an orphan!'

'Oh, right,' says Alistair, looking glum.

'Sorry, man,' says Jack, abashed.

'It's fine. I never even knew them. They died when I was a baby,' explains Alistair.

'I never knew my birth parents, either,' Filomena tells them.

'Those aren't your parents?'

'They are. But they're not my biological parents. I was adopted,' she explains.

Alistair nods. 'I wish someone had adopted me.'

'Someone did,' says Jack. 'Me.'

Alistair laughs.

Meanwhile, Jack wishes Filomena were more enthusiastic about going back to Never After with them. *You'd think she'd at least be curious about it*, he reflects. But at least now she doesn't seem to keep questioning their very existence. Jack is patient, but if he were being honest, he'd say it was getting old, trying to prove he was really there, alive, in front of her all the time.

'OK, so now you know our story. Are we done?' asks Alistair. 'Can you help us hunt for cheeseburgers now? Yesterday we couldn't find any.'

'You haven't eaten since yesterday?' she asks.

'No,' says Alistair, whose stomach growls loudly as if to agree. 'Pardon.'

'We found a few things people left in these big bins,' Jack says. 'Some kind of cheesy bread?'

'You ate trash pizza,' says Filomena, trying not to gag.

'Trash pizza – is that some sort of delicacy?' Alistair wonders.

'Where did you sleep?'

'There's a meadow not far from here,' says Jack with a shrug. 'It was quite adequate.'

'Um, no. We really need to get you guys something to eat,' says Filomena, who looks like she's starting to regret running away from him yesterday.

Jack and Alistair saw the big house she calls home. It sure looked comfy. They argued all night over ringing the doorbell, especially when it had started to rain.

'Yes! Eat!' says Alistair.

'No time. We need to get back to the tree as soon as possible,' argues Jack. 'And we were hoping you could point us in its direction.'

'Oh right, because I have the tree on my backpack,' says Filomena. 'Unfortunately, I have no idea where the tree might be.'

'None?' Alistair gasps.

'Nada. I told you I thought the books were fiction. Fantasy.'

'Yes, yes, fiction, fantasy, all the *F* words,' says Alistair. 'I learned a few more . . . They have four letters.'

'But if you went through the tree to get here, don't you remember where it is?' she asks.

'It was dark!' Alistair says defensively. 'And we were running for our lives! Excuse us if we didn't take notes.'

'I thought I knew where it was, but we kept getting further and further away,' says Jack, feeling embarrassed to admit it. Filomena seems to think he's some kind of hero, and he'd hate to disappoint her.

'Do you remember anything about it at all?' she asks.

'I remember there were letters against the hill. Tall ones,' he replies.

'Olly . . . something,' says Alistair.

'Olly?' Filomena repeats. 'Hmm . . .'

'And we were on a hillside, high above a village,' says Jack.

Filomena looks like she's deep in thought when a spark of recognition lights up her eyes. 'Olly . . . Holly . . . Hollywood? The Hollywood sign! Were you near the Hollywood sign?'

'Is that how you say it?' Alistair says.

'How would you say it?' Filomena spells it out. 'H-O-L-L-Y-W-O-O-D.'

'Hollywood. Right,' says Alistair.

'I know where it is,' she tells them. 'Let's go. Oh, wait! First, we should hunt down those cheeseburgers. There's a place not far from here.'

Chapter Ten

Pie 'n' Burger, Pied and Pipe

Filomena takes them to the Pie 'n' Burger, one of the oldest restaurants in the adjacent and much larger town of Pasadena. (Yes there is a Pasadena, a North Pasadena, and a South Pasadena, but she thinks one of them might be fictional.) At the diner she chases down three delicious cheeseburgers, as well as generous helpings of pie. Jack declared the meal as good as a giant's feast.

Afterwards, Filomena used her saved-up allowance money to hire a cab to take them to the Hollywood Hills, where the sign is located.

'Most people think of Los Angeles as Hollywood, and

Hollywood as a place where movies and television shows are made. I don't think you guys have those in Never After, do you? It's like make-believe things that people watch to pass the time,' she tells them when they're comfortably seated in the back seat of a taxi.

'Like puppet shows!' says Alistair.

'Yeah, sort of,' says Filomena. 'But, anyway, Hollywood isn't just where they make movies or, um, puppet shows. It's a neighbourhood, just like North Pasadena, where I live.'

Jack looks out the window thoughtfully. 'Like a different village.'

'Exactly!' says Filomena, pleased.

It takes about an hour to get to their destination, and when they arrive it's a long hike on foot to the top of the hill near the Hollywood sign. The three of them peer up at the sign.

'Yup, that's it. That's where we landed,' says Alistair.

'I knew you'd know the way to the portal,' says Jack with a smile.

Filomena smiles back, even though she doesn't feel as if she's accomplished anything great, but it's nice to be appreciated for once.

Jack leads the way, walking quickly through the

brush while Alistair huffs behind him.

Filomena checks the time and is relieved that it's not as late as she thought. She can get back to school for pickup at the usual hour, and her parents won't suspect anything. She turns off her phone during school hours – students aren't allowed to use their phones at school – which is convenient. If her mother were watching the tracker on her phone, she would surely have freaked out to see that Filomena is miles away from school, where she should be, and Filomena doesn't like worrying her parents.

One time she wasn't at school for the usual 3 p.m. pickup, and her parents almost had a meltdown. They'd forgotten she had band practice. What if she gets back late today? She can picture them now, running around the house, then the neighbourhood. All the calls they'd make to all the parents they know who have children at her school.

At least her list of friends isn't long, so they won't have an abundance of phone calls to make. In that way, her antisocial behaviour and apparent inability to form genuine friendships is finally coming in handy. You're welcome, Mum and Dad!

Filomena's thoughts are disrupted as she trips over a rock. Jack catches her arm just as she's about to fall, and their eyes meet for a moment. Shyly, they both look away.

When they arrive in front of the sign, Alistair sits on the curve of one of the *O*s and wipes his forehead.

'So where's the tree?' asks Filomena.

Jack waves towards a particularly large and shady oak, but neither of them seems to be in any hurry to head towards it.

'So I guess this is goodbye, then,' says Filomena tentatively.

'Uh, not quite,' says Jack.

'We lost the key to the tree,' explains Alistair.

'The Pied Pipe! That unlocks the portal! Of course!' says Filomena joyfully. Until Alistair's words set in and joy turns to aggravation. 'What do you mean, you lost it?'

'It fell from my pocket when we got here,' says Jack, looking around at the dirt and grass. 'We just have to find it, and then we'll be on our way.'

'OK, well, good luck, then!' says Filomena.

Alistair looks stricken. 'You're leaving us?'

'Um, yeah. Do you have any idea how grounded I'm going to be if I don't get back to school in time for my mom or dad to pick me up?'

She doesn't even know if she has enough money to pay for another cab ride home. She might have to take the bus.

Come to think of it, they probably should have taken the bus on the way here.

As curious as she is about Never After, she's also a bit afraid of the whole thing. While she's accepted that Jack and Alistair are real, part of her is still unconvinced that *everything* about Never After is real. Besides, her parents would want her safely back home, not traipsing around some fantasy land.

But as she backs away, she notices Jack pulling what looks like a small glass marble out of his pocket. It begins to transform in his hands, stretching and changing and shifting shape, making all sorts of funny noises until it settles into its true shape and he sets it over his left eye.

It looks like an ordinary brass telescope, the kind of thing her dad would buy on a hobby website. Except Jack is pointing it not to the sky but at the ground. When he swings it in her direction, she can see a large open eye staring at her from the glass. It's not grey, like Jack's eyes. It's golden.

'That's a Seeing Eye!' she breathes. She's only ever read about it and can't hide her delight – here it is, in real life! She stops walking backwards away from them and instead walks closer to Jack to get a better look at it. Maybe if she hovers, he'll offer her a peek.

'Ahem,' she says, clearing her throat three times.

Except of course boys never notice the obvious. Jack keeps using the magical telescope to sweep over the landscape, oblivious.

Finally, Filomena speaks up. 'Hey, can I see that?' She's trying to sound cool and nonchalant, definitely *not* like the hyperventilating superfan she is in her heart.

'Oh, sure,' he says. 'Just be careful with it, please. It's our only hope of finding the Pied Pipe. There's too much brush here. It's way too dense. But this thing should be able to find it if it's close. After all, its glass is made of—'

'Stardust,' Filomena says, finishing his sentence. 'I know, and I know how precious it is. I read all the books, remember?'

She lifts it to her eye and peers through the glass. It looks heavy and chunky, but in reality it's delicate, made of pearls and stardust, so wispy and weightless you could place it on a butterfly's wing with ease.

'It has to be around here,' says Jack, who doesn't seem all too worried, just like in the books when he's presented with terrifying obstacles.

'The Pied Pipe will only show itself if it wants to be found,' Filomena whispers to herself as she swings the Seeing Eye over the immediate terrain.

Like Jack, Filomena is not discouraged, but when she spots something small and flute-shaped glimmering with light on the ground not too far from the tree, she's so astonished that she almost drops the thing. 'I saw it! The Pied Pipe! It's over there!' she says, handing the Seeing Eye back to Jack.

He takes it and puts it up to his own eye and nods. 'Good work. It's hiding right over there! Let's go!'

He starts moving forward with steady and determined steps, pausing to gaze through the Seeing Eye every few feet, Alistair and Filomena close behind.

'I don't see it,' Alistair says.

'That's because the Pied Pipe has a mind of its own, Alistair,' Filomena tells him. 'It can hide, or it can show itself if it wants to be found.'

'Exactly,' says Jack. 'Stubborn thing, probably doesn't want to go home just yet.'

Sure enough, the pipe keeps hiding in and out of vision as they walk closer to the tree, but Jack's got a lock on its location and jumps on it before it can hide again.

'Aha!' he says, holding up the pipe as the Seeing Eye transforms back into a small marble and he puts it in his pocket. 'Will you do the honours?' he asks Alistair.

Alistair beams and puts the flute to his lips.

But before he can play a note, a loud boom of thunder crashes in a proximity too close for comfort, and a lightning bolt zaps Jack Stalker where he stands. Alistair and Filomena duck down, covering their heads. The haunting, menacing cackling begins, escalating into mad screeching and ear-piercing howls.

'She's back!' cries Alistair.

'It's just her malice!' wheezes Jack, writhing on the ground, his vines blackened and smoking. 'We're near the portal and she can sense us!'

'Jack!' Filomena cries, running to his side.

'We gotta get out of here!' says Alistair as more thunderbolts crash all around them.

'Open the portal!' Filomena yells. '*Hurry!*'

But Alistair is frozen, gaping at the flames. He's too frightened to think, and the flute trembles in his grasp.

Filomena grabs the Pied Pipe from his hands and lifts it to her lips. Without thinking, she plays the first tune that comes to mind: the theme from the movies based on the Never After books, of course. Sure enough, it unlocks the Heart Tree.

Before she can think about whether it's a good idea, she's helping Alistair bring Jack through the portal, and all three of them are hurtling into the darkness.

Chapter Eleven

Never After

Reading all the books in the world couldn't have prepared Filomena for the descent into not just another world, but a world she has seen so vividly in her imagination. She wasn't even ready – or willing – for the departure. She took not just a leap but a *lunge* of faith, if you will. One giant leap for Filomena-kind. A footstep fuelled by fear and desperation. A moment in time she can never take back. A chapter in a life story that if told would never be believed.

By the way, how late is it now? Her poor parents – she hopes her mother has anxiety medication on hand.

There's no time to think, because as she falls through the void, she feels what she can only describe as galaxies encompassing her. But words don't exist in this plane, only thought and image and memory. The word *stop* comes to mind, if she still has one.

She was swallowed into a tree.

And just as quickly another tree spits her out.

When she tumbles out of the portal, she lands on the ground with a thud, falling hard on her backside. Ouch!

Her cheeks burn, thinking of the many times she's fallen before.

Oh, has she fallen!

There was the time she fell spectacularly in gym class during dodgeball when she was trying to, well, dodge the ball. Isn't that the point?

She's heard about her slow-motion stumble and subsequent fast-forward lurch so many times that she could have written a book about it, thus becoming the third and youngest author in the family. However, she's chosen to spare herself further embarrassment by not elaborating on her 'epic spill' (as it went down in history), and instead listening humourlessly to tales told by her peers about it, complete with tear-filled eyes and fits of laughter.

And that was just one incident. She'll keep the others to herself, thank you.

She surveys her surroundings for any witnesses who may crack jokes about this later. But Alistair and Jack aren't laughing; they're dusting themselves off and making sure they have all their limbs.

Jack walks over and extends his hand, which she gratefully accepts. 'You all right?' he asks her as he helps her to her feet.

'Yes, I think so. Are you?' Filomena responds, inspecting him for blood or obvious injury from the burns he suffered in the ogre attack mere moments before they arrived here.

'Fine, thanks. Nothing a little pixie spit can't fix,' he says with a grin, shaking a tiny bottle in front of him before putting it back in his pocket.

'Cool,' says Filomena.

Once she's standing upright, she takes a deep breath and looks around. So this is Never After. *This is Never After!* This so makes up for the thirteenth and final book never being published. Understatement of the century.

She's here.

Inside the pages of the book.

Living the pages of the book.

She's here!

In Never After!

It's glorious! It's incredible! It's as if she's walked on to a movie set, except everything is real, not just a prop. It even smells better here, like just-baked bread and fresh strawberries. It smells clean and new and sparkling. It's . . . like a fairy tale. The land of fairy tales. Where dreams live happily ever after, er . . . *never after*, because, as the author explains, there's never an after here.

The dew glistens like diamonds on the grass; each petal on each flower is a precious marvel. There are colours here that she's never seen before, colours that don't exist in the spectrum back home. Is that a yellow-pink? An indigo-cinnamon?

Then she sees more: a structure made of golden straw, clearly an abode of sorts. If the wind blew . . . Wait a minute – she recognizes it from somewhere. The dwelling next to it consists of sturdy wooden sticks. The third, made of red and brown bricks. She claps her hands as three quarrelling pigs walk out of the brick house.

'Now, when he arrives, you need to get to my house immediately,' the pig in a banker's suit and tie chides his laconic brothers – one wearing a kaftan (straw dude) and the other in tartan flannel and jeans (sticks) just like from the books.

Filomena looks around for the Big Bad Wolf, a slight panic building in her chest. She's far too young to be mauled or eaten! But she's distracted when she finds what looks like the Three Bears' cottage close by. The dead giveaway is the three chairs sitting out front: one small and hard; one a bit too large and pillow-y and cloudlike; and one, in the centre, whose size and cushioning look . . . *just right*. She sniffs the air for a whiff of porridge, then continues to look around.

Nearby sits a tall tower with a peaked roof and an open window at the very top. Its beams are tree trunks wrapped in moss and vine. Filomena waits for Rapunzel to let her hair down, hoping to see if it can actually touch the ground. The top of the tower is so high, probably at least eighty feet in the air. But Rapunzel is keeping her hair to herself today, it seems.

Further away is a decrepit and seemingly abandoned castle, left to the elements, except from behind its walls comes a terrible roaring. The castle of the Beast! Filomena shivers. She hopes Beauty is on her way to save him.

Filomena turns round again. From this hillside, she can see so many castles all over the landscape – one by the sea, one by the forest, one by the city. Would that be the mermaid princess's, Snow White's and Cinderella's?

Alistair eventually disrupts her examination and thoughts by making an obvious coughing noise, and she briefly wonders how long she's been standing there, lost in wonderment.

'Still think it's not real?' he asks with a cheeky grin.

Filomena considers the question for a moment before finally saying, 'No, I no longer question whether it's real. I do, however, question what *has* been real my whole life.'

It's too late to worry about how her parents might react to her lateness. The deed is done. She's already gone somewhere they'll never be able to find her. Forget about being grounded; when she goes back, she'll never be able to leave home again.

'So?' asks Jack, eyes merry.

'It's marvellous,' she tells him.

'Welcome to Never After,' he says.

'Now go home,' says Alistair. A pause. 'Just kidding.'

Prologue

The Unseen

On the day of the christening, mere moments after the thirteenth fairy arrived uninvited and unannounced, an ill-omened quiet filled the room. The crowd was hushed and waiting, all eyes on King Vladimir, Queen Olga and the fairy Carabosse.

The tales told of this day speak of an evil spirit, of a vengeful fairy bent on revenge for her exclusion.

The tales told of this day are untrue.

Carabosse cradled her niece, the one and only princess Eliana, petting the child's precious head. She took one of Eliana's fingers in her own, admiring her beauty, and the babe wrapped her little finger round her aunt's.

The tales told of this day say that Carabosse cursed the child. That she proclaimed that the child would grow to be sixteen, only to prick her finger on a needle and sleep for a hundred years.

The tales told of this day are untrue.

Carabosse held her sweet niece in her arms, leaned down and breathed in the soft baby hair, the sweet baby down. Her sisters had already given the child their blessings. *A thousand and one blessings I bring to the child*, said her aunt the storyteller. *I wish you a party to end all parties*, said another.

It was her turn.

What blessing would she give the princess? Beauty? Health? Riches? She had all of those already.

'My darling child, I bless you . . .' She was about to murmur a spell, one that would bring happiness to the little princess for all her days, when she had a vision . . . a vision she could not *unsee* . . .

A terrible vision of a terrifying future.

The vision faded, and Carabosse stared down at her niece in her arms. How long had she stood there, watching this dark future unfold? If only there were some way she could protect her niece from the impending doom and oversee her safety for all eternity.

There was so little time.

So little time to change things.

But time was all she had.

Up on the throne, Queen Olga watched with a growing irritation, impatience plain on her beautiful face. She was about to rise in fury, but King Vladimir held his arm out to stop her. She remained seated; however, she would not bite her tongue, not even if the king ordered her to.

'Give me back my child,' Queen Olga demanded imperiously. 'Now!'

'No! Not until I've cursed her!' cried the fairy Carabosse. 'Not until I've cursed you all!'

The court reeled and gasped.

The evil fairy, cursing the princess! Cursing the kingdom!

Because Carabosse knew she had only one gift left to give, one final blessing to bestow on the child, one last chance to save her beloved sister's baby . . . And her gift was both a blessing and a curse.

Part Two

Wherein . . .
The author of the books is revealed.
The Battle of Vineland commences.
The Mark of Carabosse is discovered.

Chapter Twelve

Jack's Journey

'Come on, let's go,' says Jack, striding purposefully down the hill and away from the tree that disgorged them not unlike the one back in – what did Filomena call it? – the Hollywood Hills.

'Where are we going?' asks Filomena.

'Vineland, where I'm from,' he tells her. 'It's east of Westphalia and south of Lankershim. Bit of a trek, but if we go now we should make it before sunset.'

Alistair suddenly looks nervous, and Jack wishes he wouldn't do that. He doesn't want to scare Filomena – who seems so captivated by everything – just yet. But

Filomena, Jack is beginning to notice, is nothing if not observant.

'What happens after sunset?' she asks.

'The ogres . . .' begins Alistair. Jack gives Alistair a sharp look, and Alistair's voice trails off into silence.

'What do the ogres do?' Filomena wants to know.

'Nothing, nothing,' says Alistair. 'We'll be safe before sunset, so there's nothing to worry about.'

'Right,' says Jack grimly. 'Come on.'

Filomena looks as if she wants to ask more questions, but seems to understand the imperative of getting where they need to be before it gets too dark. Maybe she's familiar with Never After's foul monsters and assorted villains from those books of hers. Jack wonders about that book again – from what he saw of it, it had to have been written by someone from Never After. But how did it get to the mortal world? And what does it mean that the last of the series was never written? He's not sure, but he hopes Zera will be able to figure it out, which is why he's taking Filomena to her.

To Jack's relief, Alistair and Filomena are hurrying as fast as they can after him down the marked path. On the way, he greets and nods to various friends and acquaintances, all the while making it clear he doesn't have time to make conversation: Little Miss Muffet looking cross, Thumbelina and her flower prince riding on the back of a swallow, a farmer leading a cow who asks Jack if he still has those magic beans (duh, no), and several cut-rate genies offering wishes at a discount.

'One wish! Just one wish!' wheedles a purple genie floating by their side. 'One free wish! Just for you! I might throw in another one or two! You know you want to! What's your wish? What's your wish? Your wish is my command!'

'No, thank you,' says Jack, ushering his group away before any of them can fall to temptation.

Alistair looks at Jack pleadingly, but Jack shakes his head: *No.*

When they're safely away from the peddling genies, Jack exhales.

'There seem to be genies everywhere. What makes Aladdin's so special?' asks Filomena.

'Aladdin's genie lived in the lamp for thousands upon thousands of years and is the oldest and most powerful genie in all of Never After. These guys are babies compared to him. If Aladdin's genie could grant you a kingdom, the most these guys can give you is a privy.'

'Don't you have to open their bottles first before they

103

grant your wishes?' says Filomena.

'Not always. Sometimes they're just bored or mischievous,' Jack explains. 'Wishes can cause havoc. Even small ones.'

'In the books the rules are super clear,' says Filomena.

'But real life is different from books, isn't it?' says Jack.

'You have a point,' she concedes.

For a moment Filomena seems to have forgotten her great desire to return before school is over, and Jack is grateful. But no, when they're almost halfway there, she begins to fret.

'Wait! Where are we going? Why am I going with you? I need to get back,' she says.

'Not yet. You haven't met Zera,' Jack says. 'After you meet her, I'll take you back to the portal. Promise. But you need to meet her first.'

'Zera?' says Filomena. 'You mean Scheherazade?'

'You know her too?' asks Alistair, delighted.

Jack is glad that he doesn't have to explain who Scheherazade is as Filomena seems to be more than knowledgeable about her. She begins to recite a poem:

'Thirteen Fairies were born to the Fairy King and Queen.

Esmeralda, Antonia, Isabella, Philippa, Yvette and Claudine.
Josefa, Amelia, Colette and Sabine.
Beautiful Rosanna, who married the King.
Clever Scheherazade, who spun a thousand and one dreams.
And uninvited Carabosse, who was the thirteenth.'

Alistair coos. 'Ooh, I like it.'

Even Jack had to smile. 'Don't tell me: it's from the books, isn't it?'

'Yup, it's in the front of each one.' Filomena nods, then looks concerned. 'Wait, doesn't Zera live in the kingdom of Parsa? At the end of book three, when she finishes her tales, the sultan marries her. What's she doing in Vineland?'

Jack's brow furrows. 'Zera fled into exile. The ogres have been marching across Never After, taking kingdom after kingdom. One by one they fall, forced into surrender and submission. Zera took refuge in Vineland after they invaded Parsa.'

Filomena turns pale.

'When we left, the capital was crawling with ogres intent on finding Aladdin's lamp,' Jack says, his voice trembling a bit. 'There are only a few free kingdoms left – Eastphalia, Vineland, the Deep, to name a few – since the

105

surviving fairy tribes went into hiding.'

'How many kingdoms are still free?' she asks.

'No one knows. Zera's been trying to get in touch with all of them, but it's been difficult. They say Queen Olga has spies everywhere.'

'Oh my, is that Westphalia?' asks Filomena, pointing to a faraway kingdom surrounded by a thorny wall of vines that reach as high as the castle towers. The entire kingdom is cut off, covered by bramble and bristle. 'What happened?'

'Doesn't it say in those books of yours?' asks Jack.

Filomena shakes her head. She tells him what she knows, what was written: that the evil fairy Carabosse cursed the baby princess and wreaked havoc on the kingdom. But that's where the tale ends.

Oh, she's heard the usual stories: about the spindle and the curse of sleeping death and all of that. But Filomena reads the Never After books to find out the *real stories*. What happened to Princess Eliana? What happened to the evil fairy Carabosse? What really happened in Westphalia?

She waited a year to find out what happens next, and instead the book wasn't published.

'Westphalia fell on the day of the princess's christening thousands of years ago. It was the beginning of the end,'

Jack tells her. 'The princess was supposed to bring peace and hope to the kingdom. Instead it all went bad after Carabosse delivered her curse. Some say she turned the queen into a monster, but others say Olga was an ogre all along. No one knows the truth. And no one's seen or heard of King Vladimir since, much less the babe. Everyone blames Carabosse. They say this is exactly what she wanted to happen, that she was probably working with the ogres all along,' Jack says bitterly.

'That's it?' Filomena asks.

'That's it,' says Jack. 'Ever since the christening, Queen Olga has been obsessed with finding the princess. She's tried the Ring of Infinity and the Magic Mirror to look for her.'

'Why does she want the princess so badly?'

'There's some sort of prophecy around the princess's return. That she'll bring death to the ogres,' says Jack.

'No sign of her anywhere, though,' says Alistair. 'Prophecy schmophecy. It's been forever. The princess is gone.'

'Anyway, now Olga's fixated on the lamp. We tried to stop her from getting it, and the ogres chased us right off a cliff,' says Jack.

'Wait – before you came to my world, you fell off a

cliff?' she asks. It's the exact same scenario as the end of book twelve.

Jack nods. 'I told you, we were running away and stumbled into your world.'

Filomena is so shocked she can't speak. *I'm in the book. I am in the thirteenth book.*

This is the story. It's being written before her eyes.

But what happens now? Jack Stalker is supposed to rescue the princess and set things to rights so that everyone lives happily in Never After.

But will he?

Jack looks up at the darkening sky. 'Come on. We should hurry.'

Chapter Thirteen

Filomena's Journey

'Are we almost there? We've been walking forever.'
Filomena's backpack feels as if it's getting heavier
and heavier on her shoulders with each step she takes.
Her legs are growing more tired by the minute. She
feels her stomach rumble, reminding her that it's been a
long time since they hunted down those cheeseburgers.
She's been quiet, thinking about what Jack told her
about the latest events in Never After. Of course, she
should have expected it. It's in the books, after all, but
she didn't realize it was *real*. That the war against the
ogres is real. Evil Queen Olga is real. Which means

Filomena is actually in real danger here.

Grave danger.

Filomena has had so many irrational fears that it's difficult to face a rational one. She should be quaking in her boots, terrified that another Ogre's Wrath will come out of the blue. But instead she's mostly exhausted and hungry and too tired to feel frightened.

'Yeah, we're almost there. It's just around the bend ahead,' Jack says.

'Thank moons,' replies Alistair. 'Me legs're about to give out. I hope Zera's made her tulip cake.'

Filomena scrunches her nose even as she's glad that Alistair's distracted her from impending death via ogre strike. She's hungry, but . . . she's not so sure about eating flowers. 'Tulip cake?'

Alistair looks at her, agape. 'Surely you've had it before?'

She shakes her head in response. 'I mean, I've read about it, obviously. But where I'm from, we don't typically eat flowers. I have heard of rose-flavoured tea, though. Mum says it's weak. She prefers the "hard stuff". Proper English tea.'

Alistair lets out a hearty chuckle and playfully slaps her arm. 'Rose-flavoured tea! That's a good one!'

'It exists!'

'I'm sure it does,' says Alistair. 'And you saying you don't eat flowers!'

'I don't.'

Alistair laughs harder. 'As if I'd believe that!'

'I think she's serious, Alistair,' Jack says.

Alistair stops laughing almost as quickly as he started, and his face contorts into an appalled version of itself. 'Wh-what? Why? The options are limitless. There are so many delicious flowers. So many petals. The juices. The flavours. The healing properties. Not to mention the potions and the magic in them!'

'Alistair!' Jack interrupts. 'Don't make her feel bad. She's never been here, remember?'

'Sorry,' Alistair says. 'I just can't believe it. I wouldn't want to live in a world where you don't eat flowers. White orchid pastries are one of my favourite treats. Oh, almost there, Fil. That's Zera's cottage over there.'

She looks ahead of her, then looks around in every direction, but there's no cottage in sight. 'Alistair, I think you're suffering from heat exhaustion or something. Or maybe you're seeing a mirage. There's no cottage here.'

'What do you mean?' huffs Alistair. 'It's right in front of you!'

'Filomena can't see Zera's cottage. It has the glamour around it, remember?' Jack looks at Alistair as if his friend should know this.

'Ohhhhhh yeah,' Alistair says. He turns to Filomena and shrugs. 'Sorry. Forgot you're not immune to glamour yet.'

'How do I get im—' she starts, but Jack interrupts their banter.

'All right,' he says. 'Settle down.' Jack reaches out to what looks like absolutely nothing but air in front of him, knocks thrice, pauses, then knocks once more, pauses and knocks thrice more. After a few moments stretch by, he turns an invisible knob, makes an opening motion with his hand and says, 'After you.'

She still sees nothing – although she *heard* the knock sound on a solid surface – and she stares at the empty space, reflecting on how strange he looks holding an imaginary door open for her. Then he leans against nothing, shoulder pressed on a surface she can't see, and she can't believe he hasn't fallen over already.

'Go on,' Alistair encourages her, gently pushing her forward.

'Go where, exactly?' she wants to know.

'Inside, silly,' Alistair says.

But her feet don't move. She's frozen where she stands, terrified to accidentally fall through another portal without warning. 'I don't know about—'

With a friendly shove (thanks to Alistair), Filomena lurches forward and trips over what feels like a step she didn't see. Or *couldn't* see, rather. She stumbles inside, landing in a heap on the floor of a tiny foyer. She looks at the surface that's suddenly appeared beneath her, touching the wooden planks with her hands to make sure the floor is real. She's too shocked by the sudden change in atmosphere.

I was standing in front of nothing . . . There was nothing there . . . nothing at all . . . and now I'm inside a cottage.

It's one thing to read about spells and glamours and mirages, and quite another thing to experience them.

Meanwhile, the cottage glows with a warm amber light, and the scent of something sweet wafts up her nose. Ahead is a long wooden table, with places set for four. Four plates on the table. Four goblets. Four white linen cloths, folded neatly to shape the initials of each of their first names. J for Jack. A for Alistair. F for Filomena. Z for Zera.

They are expected.

Chapter Fourteen

The Cottage

'Hello?' a female voice calls out. 'Jack, is that you?'
'Yes, it's me,' Jack answers, stepping inside the room.

He offers a hand to Filomena to help her up – something recurring a bit too often already – and Alistair does the same, offering his assistance as well.

The two boys hoist her on to her feet in one fluid motion, and she turns round to see Scheherazade standing in the foyer. The sultan's queen is a young woman with hair the colour of night and a smile as soft as a crescent moon. She's dressed in a djellaba, harem pants and slippers made of the finest silk. Her forehead is studded with jewels, golden bracelets circle up her arms and there is a tiny, perfect ruby on her nose. Like her sister Rosanna, she was made mortal by marriage, but the transition did little to dampen her magic.

Thirteen fairies were born to the Fairy King and Queen . . .
Clever Scheherazade, who spun a thousand and
one dreams . . .

'Welcome,' says Zera, bowing her head to the three of them. 'Jack, Alistair, it is good to see you safely back from your quest.'

Jack bows. 'We believe the lamp is safe for now,' he assures her.

'As safe as can be,' adds Alistair.

'And you have brought us a guest,' says Zera.

'Filomena Jefferson-Cho,' says Filomena. 'Of North Pasadena.' She wonders if she should kiss Zera's hand or shake it, but curtsies awkwardly instead. 'Pleased to make your acquaintance, Queen Zera,' says Filomena, a bit awed by the dazzling beauty and power contained in the storyteller's presence.

'Oh, we don't stand on ceremony here. Call me Zera

– everyone does,' says Zera. 'You must have had a most tiring journey. Come, please, all of you,' she says, leading the way to the table. 'Supper is almost ready.' Wonderful heady smells of freshly baked bread and sizzling butter and onions emanate from the kitchen.

'Supper!' says Alistair happily. 'Thank you, Z.'

'My pleasure! I hope you're all hungry.' She takes the seat at the head of the table, with the napkin folded into a *Z*, and unfolds it and rests it upon her lap.

Filomena, Jack and Alistair take their assigned seats labelled with their names, the napkins folded into the first letter of same, and Filomena hangs her backpack on the back of her chair before sinking into it.

'How did you know we were coming?' she asks, once they are all seated.

Zera holds up her own Seeing Eye. 'I wanted to make sure you guys were safe, so I kept one of these on you. I saw you helped Jack and Alistair get away. You know the spells. And you have a certain book.'

Filomena nods.

'May I see it?'

Filomena hands it over. 'The series is really popular where I'm from, because the books are new versions of the usual fairy tales. They claim to be the "real" stories.'

'There are "usual" fairy tales?' asks Zera.

'Well, I mean, like, in other fairy-tale books, it says that the sultan was going to kill you like he killed all the other girls, except you told him all these stories and he begged for you to finish them and so at last he decided to let you live and married you.'

'I suppose that is one way to look at it,' says Zera. 'Except that isn't quite the whole truth. He was not at all bloodthirsty, and he didn't kill any of his brides. But it was such a shame for the girl's family if he rejected her that lies were told about their deaths so they could start over elsewhere. In fact, we fell in love before the first night was over. I told him the stories out of love.'

'That's exactly what it says in this book!' Filomena claps her hands excitedly.

'Interesting,' says Zera as she continues to page through the book. 'It's all here, what's been happening.' She turns the book over in her lap and gasps. 'It can't be!'

'What is it?' Filomena asks as Zera pulls the book closer to her eyes and gasps again.

'Do you recognize her?' Zera asks Jack and Alistair, holding up the back of the book so they can see the author photo.

'I think so . . . It's *her*, isn't it?' says Jack.

'Cassiopeia Valle Croix. Cassiopeia was always her favourite star,' Zera murmurs. 'Valle Croix? Loosely translated, it means "of the ancient crossways". Our home.'

'Excuse me? Who are you talking about?' Filomena demands.

'My sister,' says Zera simply.

'Your sister?'

'The author of this book is my sister who disappeared thousands of years ago,' Zera tells them.

Filomena's mind is racing. 'Your sister is Cassiopeia Valle Croix?'

'I suppose that's what she's calling herself now, or at least in your world,' says Zera. 'But I know her by her real name. The fairy Carabosse.'

'Carabosse!' shrieks Filomena. 'Your sister is the evil fairy who cursed the kingdom?'

Zera bristles. 'Carabosse was not evil. She was born to the forest, like me and all our sisters. She *had* to have a reason for what she did. Carabosse always did. I hope so, anyway.'

'She wrote these books?'

'It appears so,' says Zera with a faint smile. 'She always did think of herself as a writer.'

Chapter Fifteen

The Raid

But Jack isn't smiling. 'Carabosse was a traitor, Zera. It all began with her. She was the one who cursed the kingdom and started the war. We wouldn't be in this mess if it weren't for her. She's an evil fairy, and I'm glad she's gone.'

'I know your pain, Jack,' says Zera. 'It is mine too.'

Filomena glances over at Jack, who is brooding as he picks up his cup. 'What happened?' she whispers.

'My whole family was killed. I'm the only one left. I saw my brother burning in front of me when the ogres attacked our village,' says Jack, his jaw clenched.

Even Alistair is silent. Filomena remembers a scene from the first book – when ogres set fire to a mountain village high up in the clouds. Only a young boy survived, and he grew up to be a great hero. Jack Stalker was just a character in the book to her back then, but now he is as real as the misery on his face.

At last Zera speaks. 'And I? Is your pain greater than mine? My sisters slain and scattered? My husband murdered? Our kingdom burnt to ashes?'

Jack shakes his head, and there are tears glistening in his eyes. 'You are right. I am sorry,' he tells her.

Zera lays a hand on his arm, like an older sister. 'The ogres started this war long ago. We will fight them together and rid this land of their evil.'

Then she continues to page through the book. 'You say there are twelve of these?'

'Yes,' says Filomena. Something occurs to her that she's never noticed before. 'This book is dedicated to you.' She flips to the front matter and there it is: *For Z, don't stop dreaming.* 'All twelve of the books are dedicated to each of you, her sisters,' she adds, knowing with absolute certainty that if they went back and revisited all the other books, they would see a similar dedication in each. *For R, whom I miss dearly . . . For A, who lights up the room . . . For C, who banishes gloom . . .*

'We never knew what happened to her,' says Zera. 'After the christening. After the chaos that ensued, she disappeared. We never saw her again or knew where she went.'

'She cursed the kingdom and fled. Sounds pretty evil to me,' Alistair mutters.

'But why did she write these?' Jack wants to know. 'For mortals, no less.'

'You heard Z   she's a writer,' says Alistair matter-of-factly.

'She never wrote the thirteenth book,' says Filomena. 'It was supposed to come out. But she disappeared in my world too.'

'Yet she has not reappeared here,' says Zera. 'I wish she would. We need all the help we can get.'

'You truly believe she isn't in league with the ogres? You know as well as I that some say she is Olga herself,' says Jack, leaning so far back in his seat that his chair teeters on its hind legs and it looks as if he'll fall. But he's Jack Stalker, and he's perfectly balanced, of course.

'I don't believe it for a moment. The ogre queen is not my sister! Carabosse was one of us. She would never throw her lot in with our enemies,' says Zera. 'Like I said, there had to be reason for what she did that day.' She tenderly strokes the author photo. 'I miss her so.'

Filomena wonders if supper will ever be served, when Jack suddenly kicks his chair back into place. 'The Seeing Eye!' he says, removing it from his pocket, where it's vibrating and giving off sparks.

Zera's is doing the same, and they both look into their instruments.

'Oh no!' says Zera.

Jack leaps to his feet. The vines circling his arms tense up.

'What's going on?' asks Filomena. Alistair looks alarmed.

'It's sunset,' says Jack. 'The ogres are on the border again. This time they're hacking through our defences with some kind of vine cutter I've never seen before. They're going to break through! They'll be here soon!'

'We have to warn the others!' says Zera.

'There's no way we can warn everyone in time,' says Jack tightly. 'Even if we went house to house.'

'If only we could raise an alarm somehow!' Zera clasps her hands in despair.

Raise an alarm? Let everyone in the immediate vicinity know that they're in danger? Filomena ransacks her backpack and comes up with it. 'My emergency whistle!'

she says. 'Mum said it could wake up all of Los Angeles. It's the latest design. It's not just a whistle but some kind of megaphone recording too.'

'Can we use it?' asks Zera.

'Of course.'

'Go!' says Zera. 'Hurry!'

Filomena walks to the open window and puts the whistle to her lips. Then she turns back to them. 'You guys should cover your ears.'

She blows into the whistle, which lets out an ear-piercing, sound-barrier-destroying shriek, and when she presses a button, a deep robotic voice announces, 'EMERGENCY! EMERGENCY! THIS IS AN EMERGENCY! EMERGENCY! THIS IS AN EMERGENCY! TAKE SHELTER! THIS IS AN EMERGENCY!'

'We are indeed lucky to have you,' Zera says. Then she closes the curtains and curses vehemently. 'Sorry.'

'It's all right,' says Alistair. 'I learned some new curses while we were away. I can share them with you.'

But this isn't the time for jokes. Outside, the creatures and citizens of Vineland are running into their cottages, dens, sheds and anywhere they can find shelter, tripping over and bumping into one another as they frantically scurry for safety. Filomena sees the white rabbit almost drop his timepiece, and Goldilocks is hoofing it back to her own cottage.

'We need to prepare for battle,' says Zera. 'Follow me!'

She rushes out of the room and into her bedroom, where she bends down and picks up a floorboard that didn't look loose, and then another. She trades each of their places with the other. Then she makes quick work of moving around floorboards, rearranging them in an intricate pattern that Filomena can't quite follow with her eyes or memory. Even in her haste, Zera is graceful and elegant, as if she's done this a thousand times. Filomena fears that she has.

'I keep my weapons here,' says Zera.

Filomena feels a shudder in her bones as the realization hits her deeper this time. They are all truly in danger. What started out as awe-inspiring and a whole lot of fun has suddenly taken a dark and unpredictable turn. The panicked screams coming from outside the cottage remind her just how real this all is.

And then a familiar sound. One she never wanted to hear again. Only this time, she's not imagining it. The cackling begins again. The wicked laughter, the hysteria. The shrill and satisfied screeching.

The battle has begun.

Chapter Sixteen

The Battle

Filomena tries to remember what she knows about ogres from the books: They like to roast their victims before eating them. Ugh!

'They must know you're in Vineland,' Jack says as Zera works frantically to unlock the floorboards. 'Someone must have tipped them off. I don't think anyone would have done so willingly, but after enough pain and torture . . .'

'Someone must have cracked,' Alistair says, then shakes his head. 'I hate them. I wish they'd leave us alone. I just want this to stop.'

'Me too, Alistair. Me too.' At last, the floorboards

open and Zera begins to hoist up weapons, handing Jack a bow and arrow and removing axes and knives from the stash. 'They're here for me. And I can't leave the people of Vineland to suffer. Vineland was kind enough to give me refuge when the sultan was slain and my kingdom taken. I will not leave it to fear and ruin.'

'Neither will I,' says Jack, picking up knives and stuffing them into his boots.

Filomena feels as if she can't breathe. Outside, everything is eerily quiet. Too quiet. Everyone is hidden. Doors are shut and bolted, windows locked and curtains drawn.

Vineland is holding its breath.

Then: the sound of marching.

The ogres are on their way. In the books, the ogres are described as the ogre queen's servant-soldier hybrids, obeying her every command to destroy and cause destruction. Filomena swallows hard, telling herself to be brave. That no moment has ever mattered as much as this one is about to. Her very life may well depend on it.

Zera draws back the curtains a sliver, and through it they can see the ogre army. They're aligned in sloppy rows, for ogres don't like order, and they are snorting and stamping their feet, eager for mayhem. The ogres are even worse than described in the book: hideous, deformed, piglike creatures, with massive boils on their leathery hides that their armour doesn't cover. They're carrying steel and shields; the archers among them carry crossbows aimed at the sky, ready to rain down fire on the thatched cottages of the village.

'Do we have a plan?' Alistair asks nervously, fidgeting with his hands.

'No,' Jack says. 'But knowing we don't have a plan is better than not knowing we need one.'

'That doesn't make us feel better,' says Filomena.

'If we can bring down the general, the rest of the army will scatter,' says Zera.

'Which one's the general?' asks Alistair.

They look out of the window. 'That one,' says Jack.

An ogre the size of four ogres comes into view. This one is even uglier and meaner-looking than the rest, and wields a club wrapped in barbed wire.

'I'll use my vines to pull him off his gryphon,' says Jack.

'And I'll kill him with this,' says Zera, pulling out a silver blade from her waistband. 'Dragon's Tooth sword. Cuts through anything. My sister Antonia made this one for me.'

'You guys stay here,' says Jack. 'Stay safe. Don't do anything stupid.'

'But—' Filomena begins to protest.

'No buts,' says Jack. 'Stay here. That's an order.'

'But I know all the spells!' says Filomena. 'I can help! There are only two of you against all of them!'

She does have a point.

'She's been useful so far,' says Zera.

'See?' says Filomena triumphantly.

'We're going out there?' asks Alistair.

'No, not you,' says Jack. 'You stay inside.'

'If Filomena gets to fight, I do too,' Alistair argues. 'I'll take this,' he says, picking out a large hammer.

Seeing that Alistair won't be dissuaded, Jack gives in. 'Fine. But you guys stick close.'

He doesn't have to tell Filomena twice. She inches as near to Alistair and Jack as she can without her nose touching either of their backs, and braces herself for battle.

'Let's go,' says Jack.

For a moment, nothing happens. Everyone is tense, and no one moves.

Then Zera speaks one word: 'Now.'

And they charge out of the cottage. They huddle close together, moving forward in a cluster, but once they burst into the clearing and the line of fire, they scatter, Jack and Zera running in a zigzag manner to get to the ogre general.

Thunderbolts crackle and crash from the sky, striking

the ground with a vengeance. The ogres roar as they set cottages on fire, and when the inhabitants run out they stomp on them. They're terrifying in their size and strength, tossing creatures and fairies every which way as they crush and destroy everything in sight.

Smoke sifts into the air with a scorched scent that loiters in your nostrils, a heaviness overtaking your lungs.

Filomena thinks she hears Zera and Jack shouting out a spell, chanting together. Alistair joins in, she can hear him behind her, but she can't turn back to look at him. She's too terrified. Why didn't she agree to stay in the cottage? What was she thinking? She narrowly dodges a thunderbolt and a tree thrown in her general direction.

Filomena tries to remember the spell – any spell – but she's too rattled as an ogre stomps his way towards them, his earth-shaking footsteps approaching from behind. She's trembling as she swivels her head, unable to move the rest of her body as she stares up at the massive beast. She squeezes her eyes shut and prays he doesn't step on her or pick her up and fling her out of the the way.

But just as the ogre is about to reach them, a cry of rage rises above the mayhem.

Filomena looks up to see that Jack has used his vines to lasso the ogre general and pull him off his monstrous steed. Zera, her dark hair aflame, has leaped quickly on top of the general, her Dragon's Tooth sword held high.

'For the Forest and the Vine, the Wood and the Trees!' Zera screams. 'And for Parsa!'

With a mighty force, she stabs the ogre general right in the heart.

There is a monstrous roar, and then the ogre general explodes into a million pieces, his dark dust a cloud over the landscape.

There is a communal shriek, and all of a sudden the ogres retreat. The thunderbolts stop. The stomping foot-steps come to a halt, replaced by the sound of running.

As quickly as they arrived, the ogres disappear.

A chilling quiet stretches over what's left of Vineland, covering it like a blanket, like velvet in a casket, laying the riot to rest.

Filomena closes her eyes again and tilts her head back, breathing a sigh of relief. But, upon the exhale, she's so busy trying to collect herself and fathom what just happened that she doesn't notice the gargantuan ogre still standing there watching them, even though the others have fled.

And, at the precise moment Filomena is thanking the stars that everyone left standing is safe, Alistair is captured without a sound.

Chapter Seventeen

The Rescue

'*Help!*' Alistair screams, and Filomena turns round. Just as she believed the gruesome and relentless attack was over, it hit close to home. Alistair is in the grips of an ogre giant's fist.

Filomena looks for Jack or Zera, but they're too far away, helping creatures wounded or trapped by the attack.

It's up to her, standing small at the gigantic feet of this humongous ogre. *And I thought Algebra One Honours is hard.* She shakes her head at the silly things she'd feared before all . . . *this.*

The ogre doesn't see her; he's too busy trying to get a

good look at Alistair, the tiny boy in his mammoth fist.

Filomena hears a distinct snap, followed by a pain-stricken groan from somewhere above her.

'Ahhhh!' Alistair wails in the sky, his face contorting with agony.

The ogre brings Alistair right by his eye and roars in satisfaction. 'Got you now, you little horror!'

Alistair screams again.

Filomena can't take it any more. She has to do something to save him! She bends down and grabs a few rocks, throwing them at the ogre to try to distract him before he kills Alistair.

But the rocks bounce off his leg like pebbles. The ogre doesn't even flinch.

As much as Filomena wants to call out for Jack or Zera to help her, she knows time is ticking, and with every second that passes, another of Alistair's bones could be breaking.

She thinks back to the books. *I know all the spells*, she'd announced just moments earlier. *I can help.*

She remembers one chapter in particular where an ogre sweeps a princess off her feet, only it isn't in a good way. It was horrifying, just like this. In the book, Jack saves the princess by loosening the limbs of the ogre with a particular spell, basically turning the enemy's extremities into jelly-like appendages.

She remembers the chapter. She remembers the scene. She remembers what the princess is wearing. But the spell . . . It's on the tip of her tongue, but she can't recall where it starts or ends, or anything in between.

Alistair shrieks in pain again, and she mumbles to herself, covering her ears so she can think straight.

How did it go?

Quick. 'Ogre be quick . . .'

No . . . It went, 'Ogre, ogre . . .'

She rolls the words around in her mind a few times, rearranging them as Zera had done to the floorboards.

It comes to her all at once. She stumbles at first, attempting to remember the tongue twister's true order. But there's no time to perfect the rhyme. She decides to just spit it out and hope she gets it right. Alistair's life depends on it.

'Ogre be feeble, ogre be thick! Ogre be sluggish, ogre be sick! Ogre droop under this limbless kiss, until every bit of you is mush and twist!' she chants, over and over, until she's screaming the words into the sky. 'OGRE BE FEEBLE! OGRE BE THICK! OGRE BE SLUGGISH! OGRE BE SICK! OGRE DROOP UNDER THIS LIMBLESS KISS, UNTIL EVERY

BIT OF YOU IS MUSH AND TWIST!'

She feels her voice going hoarse as the ogre stumbles, gently at first, like he's about to sneeze. But almost instantly, before he can recover his footing, his face starts drooping. His mouth settles into a permanent frown.

His flesh goes formless, starting at the neck. What was once nimble becomes numb, the skin sagging into a gloppy substance. She watches his one arm go limp and then start flopping around like a rubber snake. Next goes the other arm, the one attached to the hand gripping Alistair.

The fist becomes fluid-like, and Alistair suddenly looks as if he's caught in a bowl of skin soup. Filomena gags while watching the transformation. The ogre is rendered powerless as his legs go next, his kneecaps turning into pure tissue and becoming formless, bending and meandering and twisting at angles that could make even the strongest stomach turn.

The giant falls to the ground in a heavy, aimless flop, his malleable body parts still detouring with a mind of their own. Filomena tries not to puke as she races to Alistair, who's still in the sloshy grip of the erstwhile powerful ogre, now a mushy pile on the ground.

Filomena climbs over the ogre, sinking into his skin as if it's quicksand. As disgusting as it is, she searches her way around the saggy, baggy sea and finally finds Alistair. She only sees his head, but she yells for him to try to reach his hand out so she can help him out of there.

He's struggling to breathe, but his hand juts out and she grabs it, pulling him out of the goop.

She groans, and yanks as hard as she can. Jack and Zera suddenly appear right behind her.

'Hey! I remember using that spell,' says Jack. 'Let me guess, that's in the books?'

'You know it! I'm a big reader, remember?' Filomena says between grunts. 'Help me get him out of here! He's drowning in bone-drool!'

Jack rushes to her side and grabs what's available of Alistair's arm, the rest still sunken in the sloppy skin-ship.

With a little help from Jack Stalker, Filomena's last tug frees Alistair from the ogre's gooey clutches, and she and Alistair go flying backwards.

She crawls towards Alistair, checking him over. Zera kneels beside her, also inspecting the boy for injury.

'Where does it hurt?' Filomena asks Alistair.

'Everywhere and after,' he says with a groan. 'But if you think this is bad, you should see the other guy.'

Filomena laughs, and they all turn their heads to the puddle of ogre, still melting by their feet.

Chapter Eighteen

The Feast

After the last of the ogres have retreated, leaving wreckage and ruin in their wake, Zera starts tending to the injured. There are too many creatures to count, bloody and hurt in the aftermath of the attack. Jack and Filomena assist her, as well as others who are unharmed, and they carry or drag as many bodies as they can to a makeshift healing centre in one of the big barns. The structure isn't totally intact, but it's sturdy enough to keep them safe and warm inside.

Zera organizes the pixies and asks them to work their magic on the wounded, healing their injuries to the best of their abilities. Some are unable to heal the others properly, due to injuries they themselves have sustained during the assault. But she remains steadfast in her mission to help the others. She tends to as many as she can, quickly and with a resolute purpose. Her grace never wavers, nor does her kindness and patience. Filomena finds herself wishing Zera were *her* big sister. No one would tease her back home if she was her protector.

Filomena sits at Alistair's bedside as Jack helps Zera take care of the others. Alistair's been healed quite well, after what appeared to be some broken ribs. But there's nothing the pixies can do for the bruising that's already started to manifest all over his body. It's an unfortunate side effect of not only the incident that required the healing in the first place, but the healing process itself. They can fix some things, but they cannot perfect or control how it takes shape.

Filomena looks at him with a sympathetic smile. 'How ya doin', bud?' she asks, purposely sounding jocular to cheer him up.

'I'm feeling better. Still quite sore, but that's to be expected when you're nearly squeezed to death by an ogre,' he replies with a smirk, and she's glad to see he hasn't lost his sense of humour in the traumatic event.

'You don't say,' she says, laughing. 'How long do you think you'll be stuck in this bed?'

'Not sure. I know I can't move around just yet. The magic takes time to work its way through the body. If I move, I could seriously hinder it and wind up with more legs than any person should have. Or, worse, something internal could go wrong. What if I could never eat again because my intestine wound up in my heart?'

Filomena shakes her head, but the thought of it frightens her, and she realizes how close they came to losing him altogether. 'I'm sure that won't happen. Just . . . stay still.'

'You couldn't trade me a hundred Lily Licks not to,' replies Alistair.

She tilts her head. 'Lily Licks?'

'Yeah, you know, the little white-and-yellow suckers? Lilies?'

She shakes her head. 'No, but what is it with you and flowers?'

'What is it with *you* and no flowers?' he counters.

Just as Filomena is about to answer, Zera's voice rings throughout the large room, and Filomena turns to listen.

Zera announces that she will be providing a feast for all the survivors, and the meal is already being prepared.

An assortment of food and drink will be served, and all are welcome to attend. She adds that although the injured have to unfortunately remain here for their own safety, dishes will be brought to them by the helpers and healers so they can eat comfortably without risking further injury. She closes her message by saying how thankful she is for everyone's assistance – and resilience – today.

Cheers are heard throughout the room, and heads (that are able to) are nodding and faces are smiling at this as she heads to get back to work.

Filomena is woken by a gentle shake. She hears a voice that sounds like Jack's.

'Filomena? Wake up. It's time to eat,' he says.

She opens her eyelids little by little. She squints at Jack, with the kind of haze and confusion one has when waking from a nap and not knowing what time, or even year, it is. She fell asleep in her chair beside Alistair's bed. He's also out, snoring away, drool dripping from his lip to his chin.

'How long was I asleep?' she asks.

'I don't know,' he says. 'You needed the rest, anyway. You didn't miss anything here. Just more of the same. But come now, – let's go eat. I'm sure you're starved.'

Jack walks her back towards Zera's cottage, which is

much larger than she remembered. 'This is almost as big as a palace,' she says. 'Oh! It's enchanted.'

'To fit as many as it needs to. Useful, isn't it?'

The table where they sat just a little while before is now a vast oak table crowded with the various citizens of Vineland. Fairies and goblins next to farmers and crofters. Filomena is famished. Plus, it'll be interesting to finally eat a meal that's not takeout.

Zera raises her goblet of wine and taps the table with her open palm three times, signalling for silence. She gives another short speech about the events of the day, once again thanking everyone for their courage during the attack and their eagerness to aid the injured so selflessly.

'We will rebuild Vineland together. And take back Parsa. And Westphalia. And Wood Vale and the Meadow Glen. Brick by brick, straw by straw, stick by stick, little by little. And in time we will flourish, in peace, safe from ogres, witches and giants. We will defeat the ogre queen and live in harmony once again. I, Scheherazade formerly of the Great Forest and of Paras, promise you this.'

She says it with such conviction that Filomena wants to believe her. But, as she listens to the speech, all she can think about is the books. And with the thirteenth book unpublished, she has no idea how the story will end. If they will, in fact, be victorious in the long war against the witches and their ogres. Where the series left off, the fairy tribes and their allies had been mostly losing this battle. She keeps her thoughts to herself and remains seated quietly at the table.

At last the food is served, 'Warm summer soup with berry bread,' announces a harried elf, plunking down a huge vat next to freshly baked loaves. There's also a large, delicious-smelling roast with mashed truffles, and a heaped plate of crispy frog fritters. Then cranberry cabbage and gooseberry prunes. Three different kinds of porridge are lined up one after another – pumpkin, peach, and persimmon. A large bowl of magical beans appears beside those, and they're jumping in the bowl as people reach in to grab some. They are served a wide array of vegetables, and Filomena has never been so happy to see broccoli and carrots in her whole life.

To drink: mulberry wine, thick cups of morning dew, and juices from every kind of fruit, including some she has only read about in the books: cherry apples, bumbleberries, and mango-nanas.

'Please, help yourselves,' Zera encourages.

Soon everyone is eating heartily.

The food is beyond delicious. The summer soup tastes

exactly like the season it's named for – hot, fragrant and full of sunshine – while the berry bread is juicy and buttery at the same time. The roast melts on her tongue, and mashed truffles are the most heavenly thing she's ever tasted.

The creatures and citizens talk in low voices that echo across the hall. A soft light fills the spacious room, now crowded with Vineland's survivors. Filomena is momentarily saddened at the occasion, wishing the cause were a celebration instead of devastation. But she's hungry, and so she does what everyone else is doing. She eats.

Chapter Nineteen

The Mark

Assorted creatures volunteer to clear the table and serve dessert. Dishes and plates are swept away by swift hands. Filomena waits in wonder, eyeing the many treats being laid out on the table in front of her. Rumple, a tiny elf, plops down a towering multi-tiered dish with all kinds of cookies. She smells the oatmeal raisin, but there seems to be another ingredient as well. Fairy dust, maybe?

The table grows heavy with cakes of all kinds: the famous tulip, but also chicory, chocolate, and goldberry rose. Further down is a variety of pastries, creating a carnival of colours in the centre of the table. She catches sight of small round white-and-yellow candies shaped in the form of a flower, and smiles. Lily Licks!

Sprouting from one of the cakes is a white orchid, and the cake is tall and layered like a wedding cake, only more intricate and beautiful. Filomena's mouth starts watering at the sight of it, and she fights the urge to lick the icing from the top. She wants to try one of everything, but she knows her eyes are bigger than her stomach.

Filomena is helping herself to thirds when Alistair shows up at the table with an easy smile.

'Hey, guys,' he says cheerily. He looks at all the desserts laid out before him and rubs his palms together. 'Oh, I made it just in time!'

Filomena looks up at him questioningly. 'Shouldn't you still be in bed? What about your intestine being shoved up into your throat?'

'First of all, I was worried it would twist into my heart if I jumped around. But I was cleared to go. The pixies did their thing, and I'm good as new. See?' Alistair says, doing a little jig and spinning at the end, landing with his hands out.

'All right, all right,' Jack chimes in. 'Go easy, will you? You were nearly squeezed to a pulp.'

Alistair makes a face.

In the meantime, Jack gets up to grab Alistair a chair, and when he returns to the table, he squeezes it in next to his seat.

'Look, Fil!' Alistair says excitedly, pointing to the small round white-and-yellow candies she noticed earlier. 'Those are the Lily Licks! You have to try one!'

'I did!' she says gleefully.

'Did you have a slice of the tulip cake too?' asks Alistair.

'I had two,' admits Filomena, who'd beenunable to resist the spongy confection iced with real yellow tulips.

'I need to catch up, then,' says Alistair.

As they eat, a bard picks up a lute and begins to serenade the gathering. Zera makes her way down the table and stops at Filomena's place.

'You did well today,' the fairy tells her.

'Thank you,' says Filomena.

'There's something about you . . . Your presence here cannot be a mere coincidence,' says Zera thoughtfully. 'The way you cast your spell reminded me of someone, and I couldn't think of who until now.'

Filomena feels shy.

'And then I realized . . . but of course! It's just been such a long time since I've seen her.'

Filomena tenses at Zera's words, and even more so

when the fairy leans ever so close to her and lifts her hand to Filomena's forehead. She can smell the lilac in Zera's hair, mixed with the subtle scent of smoke from the fires from the earlier battle.

Zera inches her open palm closer to Filomena's forehead until it's nearly touching, and she whispers, 'The thirteenth fairy is missing, my sister is she. The thirteenth fairy is hiding, won't you show her to me?'

Filomena feels something explode inside her and cries out, reaching for her forehead, which feels as if it's splitting in two.

'Uhhhh . . . what's happening?'

In reply, Zera offers her a tiny hand mirror from her pocket. 'Look for yourself.'

On her forehead, underneath the skin, is a luminescent mark: a tiny crescent moon surrounded by thirteen tiny stars.

'Wh-what is that?'

Next to her, Alistair edges back in his chair a bit as he points to her forehead. 'Is that what I think it is?' he asks no one in particular.

'It is,' says Zera, awe in her voice. 'Carabosse, what have you done?'

'What's going on?' Filomena demands, staring fixedly

at the reflection of the mark on her forehead. Is it her imagination, or does it itch a little?

'You carry the mark of thirteenth fairy,' Jack says, his mouth twisting as if it tastes bitter on his tongue. 'The fairy Carabosse.' He looks as if he wants to say something more but decides against it. He also inches away from her just a little bit.

Filomena remembers Jack's words about Carabosse. *It all began with her. She was the one who cursed the kingdom and started the war. We wouldn't be in this mess if it weren't for her. She's an evil fairy, and I'm glad she's gone.*

She stares at herself in the mirror again. 'Excuse me?'

'You are marked by the thirteenth fairy. You carry her power and her protection,' says Zara. 'I was wondering how a mortal girl could cast spells that only those of the forest can wield.'

'But what does it mean?'

'I do not know,' says Zera. 'For a moment I thought – I thought you might be her, returned to me.' She hangs her head.

'I am not Carabosse!' cries Filomena. 'Never!'

'Perhaps not,' Zera says. 'But you are connected to her somehow, and to me, and to the rest of us. It can only mean one thing: You, Filomena Jefferson-Cho, are one of us. You belong here. In Never After.'

'Ooooh,' says Alistair.

Jack kicks him under the table.

'Ouch!' Alistair glares at Jack. Jack glares back.

But Filomena hasn't said a word since Zera's pronouncement.

Because, instead of excitement, all she feels is an intense and rising anxiety. 'No. Absolutely not! I'm Filomena Jefferson-Cho of North Pasadena, and I want to go home!' She turns to Jack. 'You promised. Take me home *now*.'

Prologue

The Uneaten

The thirteenth fairy cursed the princess. She cursed the kingdom. For what did she see in her dark vision? What did she see that could not be unseen?

Carabosse saw the beautiful new queen on her throne. She saw what she had done and what she planned to do. A new princess was born, a new hope for the land. And that was when Olga formulated her evil plan.

A new maiden welcomed to the castle was she. Into Rosanna's bedroom Olga crept, and into the queen's chalice Olga dripped death. After the devious deed was done, Olga left.

The poison spread slowly at first. Rosanna's fair flesh flushed, reddening and heating until all her veins burst.

Olga comforted the king in his time of woe, holding him in her arms as he wept of his sorrow.

His now motherless daughter was asleep in her crib. Olga promised King Vladimir she'd care for the babe . Then she insisted they banish Rosanna's sister Carabosse from the kingdom – if he wanted his new love to live.

So within a few days after Rosanna passed, Vladimir took Olga as his new wife and vowed she'd be his last. It worked, the spell she had cast. Now, for some time longer, she would have to wear this mask . . .

The christening of the baby princess was a celebratory blast. The crowd was impressive, a glittering mass. But, when the new queen spotted her foe, Olga was aghast.

Eleven fairies invited, for the twelfth was dead and the thirteenth shunned. So when Carabosse strode into the christening, the whole court was stunned.

Queen Olga arose, shrieking in protest. But Carabosse lifted her baby niece, holding her close to her chest. And when she closed her eyes, this is what she saw:

Princess Eliana at sixteen, a beautiful young woman with sad eyes and a wisdom older than her years, marrying handsome Prince Stefan.

Eliana in her white gown, gorgeous and glowing, ready to be wed. Her proud parents watching from the balcony. King Vladimir all smiles. Queen Olga observing with hungry eyes.

Then later:

Eliana was older now, a mother of two. She was putting her babes to sleep in the nursery when she heard the door close, and turned round to see Queen Olga staring at her.

The queen's mouth was open.

Were those fangs?

Eliana backed away slowly. 'Mother, is that you?'

'It's me, dear. Your dearest mother,' Olga said all too cheerfully, inching forward with slow and purposeful steps, 'and you smell delicious . . . I have been waiting so long, so long for this day.'

Eliana's back hit the wall – nowhere left to retreat.

Olga expanded, transformed, morphing into her true shape. Bulbous nose, boil-covered skin, hideous and hungry. She was no longer queen or mother but an ogre.

The ogre queen of Orgdale.

Westphalia's sworn enemy.

Eliana watched in horror, stunned by her mother's transformation into such a hideous thing. Her eyes grew wide just before she screamed. A shrill cry of fright, alone and terrified. Her mother had turned into a monster before her very eyes.

The babies started to cry.

Elliana's fear turned to helplessness as she looked to the bassinet, where the twins lay. The cries doubled. The screams became shrill.

Blood on the wall.

Blood on the floor.

Then at last – an ogre fully satisfied.

For hunger like that cannot be denied.

Carabosse closed her eyes against this terrifying vision and held her baby niece in her arms. She would not leave her sister's daughter to the slaughter. She vowed that, as long as she lived, the princess would remain uneaten.

Part Three

Wherein . . .

  Filomena leaves.

  Filomena returns.

  Alistair Bartholomew Barnaby, will you please stand up?

Chapter Twenty

Back

Filomena Jefferson-Cho wakes up in her own bed in her own home. At first she doesn't realize where she is. She feels the plush down comforter around her before she fully opens her eyes. *Wait! Is she truly home finally?* Bolting upright, she looks down, recognizing the white bedspread and the light teal furry body pillow. She hears a whimper and realizes she's woken Adelina, her little Pomeranian pup.

Filomena pets Adelina and kisses her little head, scooping her up and cradling her. 'Hi, baby! I missed you so much!' The dog probably thinks Filomena is nuts.

She hasn't gone anywhere, right?

It was just a dream.

It wasn't real.

Thank Zera.

Filomena looks to her left and sees her bookshelf, the Never After books piled high on the top shelf.

She checks her arms for any scratches or bruises, for any sign that what happened was not just a dream. There's nothing. No scratches from the ogre burns, no marks from the battle. Breathing a sigh of relief, she lies back down and closes her eyes, snuggling under her blankets. She curls up into a ball and hugs the covers tight. 'It was just a dream. It was just a dream.'

She repeats the words to herself and then shakes her head, amazed at how *real* dreams can feel sometimes. When she first woke up, she would have sworn she had actually been in Never After. She would have insisted she had visited the fantasy world she's read about in the pages of her favourite books and that she'd actually met the characters from that world as if they were real people. Jack. Alistair. Zera.

Of course it was a dream, she thinks as she inches closer and closer back to dreaming. *The Never After books are just that: books. Of course they're not real. How silly to think otherwise.*

The sheer and utter disappointment of the thirteenth book not coming out was probably the cause of her dream. Yes, her subconscious emotions must have got the best of her. She drifts back to sleep, exhausted from the lucid adventure. The last thing she remembers before falling asleep again is Zera with her hand outstretched over Filomena's forehead, whispering a mysterious spell.

When Filomena wakes for the second time, it's a while later, and it dawns on her that she hasn't slept in like this in quite some time. Stretching her arms wide, she exhales the rest of her exhaustion and decides to get up before her parents question if she still has a pulse.

That's another way she knows it was all just a dream. Had she actually skipped school and gone to the Hollywood Hills and travelled through the Heart Tree portal into Never After, her parents surely would have freaked out, and there is *no way* she would have forgotten that inevitable lecture. She gets up, rubbing the sleep from her eyes, and climbs out of bed.

She catches her reflection in the mirror above her vanity and nearly falls backwards at what she sees. *No, no, no, no.* She squeezes her eyes shut and vehemently shakes her head. '*This cannot be happening. This cannot be happening*,' she repeats in a frantic whisper, anxiety filling her chest like a balloon about to burst. *I must still be dreaming.*

She pinches herself hard on her arm and winces. 'Ow!'

Trying to calm down, she convinces herself to turn round and face the mirror again. Surely she just imagined that the fairy mark was still on her forehead.

She slowly turns back towards the mirror, but keeps her eyes on her feet. When she finally summons the courage to look up, she's horrified to find that the mystical mark is definitely still visible on her forehead. There it is. The mark of Carabosse: a crescent moon with thirteen stars around it, one for each fairy. It glows beneath her skin, like she's lit up from inside.

What is happening?

She runs to her bathroom, grabs a washcloth, and starts wiping at her forehead with soap and warm water. She scrubs and scrubs until her skin is red and raw. She remains in there for almost an hour, trying to get rid of the mark. But nothing works. She tries a charcoal face mask, letting it sit for twenty minutes. But the mark is still there when she wipes the grey sludge away from her skin. She tries an assortment of tonics and lotions. Nothing works.

'Filly?' her mother calls from downstairs. 'Honey, are you up?'

'Yes, Mum!' Filomena yells back, trying to hide the

horror in her voice. 'I'll be right down!' At least it's Saturday and she doesn't have to go to school.

She looks for something to cover up her forehead, rummaging in her closet for a hat or a headband – anything to hide the fairy mark from the world. Finally she finds an old beanie and pulls it low on her head. She inspects herself in the mirror multiple times before deciding it'll have to do for now, until she figures out what in the other-world is going on.

If the mark is real, then it means everything that happened to her was real.

Let's please not have this argument about what's real and what's not again, she remembers Jack saying.

OK, then.

No argument there. The fairy mark on her forehead is definitely as real as the sunshine through the blinds.

She walks downstairs, trying to appear cool, calm and collected. Turns out she wasn't sleeping in so late after all, as her parents are still seated at the table with breakfast ready. The delivery bag sits on the counter, just as it always does. But then she looks at the time and sees it's almost noon.

'Morning, sweetheart,' her father says. 'We've been waiting for you to eat. You slept in awfully late today. Everything OK?'

159

Filomena sees the concern in his eyes, and he and her mother await her answer with the patience they've always had with her, even in her bratty moments.

She pulls her chair out and sits down slowly, hesitating to respond. She wonders how she can ask them what she's about to ask them without hurting their feelings or causing them undue concern.

'Mum, Dad, I have to ask you something,' she finally says.

Her mother looks at her affectionately. 'Of course. You can ask us anything.'

'What is it, baby?' her dad asks. 'We're all ears.'

'I know you guys adopted me when I was a baby, but do you know anything about my birth parents and where they were from?' she asks. Filomena holds her breath, anxious about what they'll say. What do they know? *Do* they know? About Never After? About what's hidden beneath this beanie she's wearing?

Her parents exchange meaningful, troubled looks, and it's quiet for a moment before they both shake their heads.

'No, honey, we don't know anything about them at all.'

Chapter Twenty-One

School Daze

The rest of the weekend is the same. On Sunday she sleeps restlessly, and when she wakes up, the fairy mark is still there. On Monday morning she once again bolts upright, sweating and shaking. Adelina Jefferson-Cho looks up at her, alarmed. Filomena exhales, telling her pup it's OK, and lies back down for a few moments, reflecting on her most recent nightmare.

She dreamed she was back at school, wearing her beanie – the same one she'd been wearing when she asked her parents about her biological parents. When the bell for the first period rang, signalling that it was time for everyone to be in class, she was still at her locker, surrounded by the Fettucine Alfredos. They were teasing and taunting her as usual, saying mean things and pushing her to the point of frustrated and tearful rage.

One of them ripped the beanie from her head, revealing Carabosse's mark. They all gasped, looking at her with revulsion, telling her they always knew she was a total loser. They said they were going to tell everyone, and one of Posy's minions snapped several quick photos for proof. Filomena screamed in response, begging them not to. She didn't even want to believe it herself, let alone have the entire school know.

But the mark was already glowing, and once Posy's minion Petunia had added a filter to it, it was even brighter, blazing in the image like some sort of blasphemous disfigurement. The photo was shared everywhere, going viral online before the end of the day. Her secret was out.

Everyone knew.

Word had got back to her parents. In her dream, they'd taken her first to a priest and then to a doctor to be evaluated.

Luckily, she woke up to find it had been just a nightmare. But the mark on her forehead is definitely still there. She grimaces as she stares at it, wondering whether, if she wishes hard enough, it will disappear. She just wants her normal, boring life back in sunny, sleepy North Pasadena.

She runs through her usual morning routine, taking a shower, brushing her teeth. She feeds her beta fish, Serafina Jefferson-Cho, squatting down to wave hello to her. Then she gets dressed in her usual school uniform: white shirt, green plaid skirt, oversized hoodie. Today she puts on her combat boots. Just in case she winds up at war with someone. The black beanie goes on last. And she adjusts it while looking in the mirror, ensuring it covers every part of the fairy mark. She considers cutting herself some bangs, but the kind of hair she has would never allow them to be easy to manage.

'Come on, Filomena,' her dad yells up the stairs. 'We gotta get going or you'll be late for school.'

'Be right there!' she yells back, grabbing her jacket and backpack and heading downstairs.

They leave the house together after she kisses her mother goodbye, and as they walk down the driveway to his car, her father looks at her curiously.

'Still wearing that beanie, huh?' he asks. 'I mean, I like it, but are you allowed to wear hats in school?'

She gulps. They both know the answer to that is no. '

I'll take it off if I have to,' she says.

He shrugs in response, and they hop into the car. When he pulls up to the school and drops her off at the kerb where he always does, she gives him a goodbye peck on the cheek, and he reminds her that he loves her.

'I love you too,' she says before she gets out of the car, adding, 'Get your word count in today,' before she closes the door and waves him off.

She takes a long breath, squares her shoulders and stares ahead at the school, praying that no one rips this beanie off her head like in her nightmare.

But to her surprise, when she walks inside and approaches her locker, the Garganelli Gang is nowhere to be found. She wrinkles her face, wondering if they've chosen to torment someone else today. *Odd*, she thinks as she dials her locker combination and opens it up.

Once she has the books and notebooks she needs for her first few classes, she closes her locker and sees the Ravioli Rodeo round the corner into the hallway. *Oh great. Here they come*, she thinks, swallowing hard in preparation for the verbal, and possibly physical, assault. If her dream *wasn't* a dream, are they going to kill her for what happened last time – when she led them on the chase and she wound up in a magic tree, out of their reach? Or was that part of the dream, too? It's so hard to tell any more.

As they approach, Posy and her minions stare at her, only it's a new kind of stare. One she hasn't seen from them before. They eye her cautiously, keeping their distance. They're quiet as they pass by her and wiggle their way down the hall like the noodles they are.

She watches them in confusion, wondering why they're not bullying her as usual. Then she realizes it's because today they can hurt her without a word.

Her best friend, Maggie Martin, is alongside them. And as Maggie's eyes meet Filomena's, she whispers something to Posy and breaks away from the group. The rest of the noodles wait and watch.

Maggie grimaces awkwardly, a not-quite-smile on her lips as she keeps about six feet of distance between them. 'Hey . . .'

'Hey,' says Filomena. She hadn't realized how much she missed Maggie until she saw her. Maggie is a big fan of the Never After books too. There's so much Filomena wants to tell her! But she can't, not with Posy and her noodles watching them. 'So, uh, you're one of the Alfredos now?'

Maggie shrugs. 'They're not as bad as I thought they were. Actually, they've been really nice to me.'

'Oh,' says Filomena, because that's all she can say.

'I mean, everyone has to grow up, right? We can't just spend all our days reading books and writing fan fiction and wearing Stalker hats,' says Maggie in a somewhat exhausted tone, as if Filomena is a child and Maggie is not just three months older.

Ouch.

'Why not?'

'I mean, everyone has to grow up sometime, Filomena. We're in *middle school* now.'

'Right,' says Filomena, since this is obvious.

'OK, then,' says Maggie.

'That's it?'

'What do you want me to say? They told me some pretty crazy things about what happened on Friday. They said you *cursed* them or something. Everyone's a little scared of you now. But that's good, right? At least they won't bother you any more.'

'I didn't curse them. I didn't do anything!' says Filomena. All she did was stop time! That wasn't a curse, was it? She wondered, thinking of what Zera had told her – that she carried the mark of Carabosse – and then how Jack had reacted to the news, how repulsed he was all of a sudden.

It's so confusing.

'Bye, Filomena.' But before walking away, Maggie takes one last look. 'Oh, and I'm sorry about the thirteenth book. I heard it didn't come out. You must be pretty upset.'

'Come on, Mags,' says Posy, tired of waiting and pulling on Maggie's sleeve. 'Let's go watch the boys play basketball.'

With that, Maggie offers an apologetic look and walks away, back to the Penne Posse. The group looks at Filomena suspiciously, like they know something is up, and Filomena gets another knot in her stomach, only this time she wonders if she's going to be sick.

They start walking down the hall again, Maggie in tow. Filomena stands there, alone, watching her now ex-best-friend walk away with her sworn enemies. She tries not to cry, at least not until they're out of sight, promising herself she'll make it to the bathroom before she's too late for class.

'Stay away from us, *witch*,' Posy tosses over her shoulder, and Filomena tugs the beanie further down over her forehead as she watches them disappear.

Chapter Twenty-Two

Back to the Books

At least Filomena survived the school day without having to remove her beanie. Her teachers didn't seem to mind, except for one who eyed her accusingly but didn't say anything. Mr Hernandez, her maths teacher, probably assumed she has lice. She saw him scratching his head during the remainder of the class, like he was paranoid he'd somehow caught the critters. But she'd rather have her teachers think she has something wildly contagious than have the entire school and world know about her fairy mark, or curse, or whatever it is.

After taking Maggie away, the Linguine Losers left her

alone for the rest of the day. They kept a close eye on her, though. At first Filomena briefly wondered if she was just being paranoid. No, she wasn't. Every time she looked up from her work or her book, there they were, staring at her. She glared back. They didn't stop staring.

To make matters more uncomfortable, she spent the whole day looking over her shoulder, half expecting Jack or Alistair to pop out and force her to go back to Never After. But they never appeared.

At long last the bell rings and school is done for the day. Dad picks her up as usual, and the minute they pull into the driveway, she races out of the car and to the front door before he even shuts the engine off. 'What's the big hurry?' he calls out.

'Oh, nothing!' she yells back. 'I just have a lot of homework to do!'

Before he can respond, she's already inside, closing the front door swiftly behind her so that the puppy can't escape.

Dad looks baffled for a moment. He's probably wondering why Filomena is acting this way, whether something happened at school or with her friends – make that *friend*, singular. She only ever had Maggie, and now she has nobody. Filomena knows she's been unlike herself the last couple of days, and Dad will probably ask her about her behaviour later, as he's really into being a good parent.

Filomena quickly says hello to her mother on the way in, then takes the steps two at a time until she's upstairs and in her bedroom. She slams her door behind her and locks it. She can't wait to get this beanie off her head! It's been itching her almost all day, and she wants to see if, by some miracle, the fairy mark is gone.

She tears off the hat and throws it across her room, where it lands on Adelina, who is trailing behind her, tail wagging. The pup lets out a small and surprised whimper as the item softly lands on her little body, and then she runs in a circle and barks at it like it's a threat.

Filomena stands in front of the mirror, tracing her fingertips along the mark that is very much still there, and very much still real.

There has to be a way to get rid of it! She can't wear a beanie for the rest of her life, like some emo dude! Then she has an idea. She runs over to her bookshelf, looking at the top shelf, where the books in the series are lined up. She thumbs through them until she finds the very first book about Never After.

If there's something – anything – she's missed, it'll be in

there, and she decides to read all the books again, starting with volume one, to search for a spell or something to get rid of this mark on her head.

Just as she settles into bed, her doorknob starts turning.

'Fil?' her dad asks. 'Honey, why is the door locked?'

'Um, no reason!' she answers nervously, rising from the bed and grabbing for the beanie on the floor. She puts it back on her head and checks the mirror, making sure the entire glowing mark is covered before seeing what her father wants.

Filomena takes a deep breath to calm her pounding heart, pasting on a fake smile and trying for somewhat-normal demeanour. 'What's up?' she asks too cheerfully as she swings the door open and leans against the doorframe. *Here it comes. Concerned parenting.* She braces herself.

Dad stands outside her room with a perplexed look on his face. 'Um, can we talk for a minute?' he asks.

'Sure,' she says, moving aside. He walks in and takes the seat at her desk, shifting her backpack out of the way. 'What's up?'

'I was going to ask you that,' he says. 'Something on your mind? The other day you asked about your biological parents out of the blue, for the first time in twelve years. I just wanted to make sure everything's OK. Is there something going on you'd like to talk about, sweetie?'

Yes.

So much. Let's start with the fairy mark on my head.

Then we can move on to how fiction isn't fiction at all.

Yes.

'No,' she says, after a moment. 'Everything's fine. I swear.'

'Really?' he prods.

She sits on her bed and looks down, fidgeting with her pillow. She can't look him in the eye and lie. 'I was just curious. You know I love you and Mum, but um . . . it'd be nice to know where I came from.'

He moves to sit next to her on the bed, putting his arm around her. 'I know, sweetheart. Mum and I love you too. So much. You are the greatest gift we could have ever received. I wish we could tell you more, but we just don't know anything.' He removes his glasses and starts wiping them with his flannel shirt.

'It's OK.'

'Are you sure? I wish we had the answers, I really do,' her dad tells her sadly.

'No, it's all right. I promise.'

'No matter where you came from, you're ours. You're Filomena Jefferson-Cho.'

'Of North Pasadena,' Filomena adds. 'I know.' She smiles.

'You're our baby.'

'I know I am.'

After a parting hug, he leaves the room, and she locks the door behind him, taking the beanie off once more.

Filomena exhales. She loves her parents, but she can't burden them with the truth. Or put them in any sort of danger. The ogre queen was able to send her wrath to this side of the portal. What if her parents were attacked?

She kicks off her combat boots and cosies up in bed, starting with page one of volume one. She even reads the stuff she normally skips, like the copyright page and printing information. She pets her puppy with her free hand as she turns the pages, and the dog snuggles up next to her. They're very cosy. No one would think there was anything wrong with this scene, or that one of them might be sporting a glow-in-the-dark evil-fairy mark.

Sometime later, after Filomena has read a decent chunk of the first book, she pauses and puts it down, scrambling through memories of previous reads. This book seems to be . . . different. She notices small discrepancies as she goes, and questions whether her recollection is simply off or if something strange is going on. The little instances are not enough to confirm or deny, though. She knows certain things get forgotten over time, especially when someone reads as often as she does. She's read many books since this one. She's just mixing up details in her mind, confusing them with other books, or possibly melding all the stories into one.

But the more she reads, the more she notices. She sits up, changes position, reading the book so closely that her nose is nearly pressed to the page.

Unless she's somehow lost her mind, she's pretty sure this isn't how the story goes.

The first book is the story of Jack the Giant Stalker. But somehow, as she rereads it, it's not.

The book couldn't possibly rewrite itself . . . could it? she ponders. Because when she reaches the part about how Jack gets his name, the story is not at all how she remembers it.

In the previous version she read – although it's the *same* copy she's always had – Jack defeats the giant. He conquers the giant, thereby receiving the nickname Jack the Giant Stalker.

She is certain about this; she would stake her life on it. Jack Stalker is the hero of the story. But in this version, this strange and unexplainable new one, the tale is changed for the worse. Jack never even overpowers the giant. Instead, he falls out of the sky. Jack dies.

Wait! Jack dies! What?!

When she finishes the passage, she gasps and covers her mouth. She puts the book down and shakes her head, trying to make sense of this. The original story is gone, erased, rewritten. It's been replaced with an entirely different version.

This book isn't the one she's read before. It's not even close. For one, it's kind of plodding. And the story seems to centre on a mean little witch who's horrid to everyone.

But what she doesn't know, or understand, is how it's possible.

This book is the *same* one she bought years ago. This is exactly the same copy – dog-eared, with her name written in ink on the front page. How is this happening?

She almost can't bear to read any further.

But along the way, she notices something else that's peculiar.

New characters are introduced in this version. And they sound like they resemble a certain Macaroni Mob a little too closely for her liking. The mean little witch has a group of trolls who do her bidding. These are the villains of the story in the original book. But now they're presented as the heroes.

What is going on here?

Filomena removes all the other Never After books from her shelf. Sure enough, there's nothing about Jack, or Alistair, or Zera, or any of the characters she knows and loves. They're nowhere to be found.

She turns back to the first book. Wait! Now even the title has changed! It used to be called *Never After: Giant Stalker*. But now the title splashed across the front cover reads: *Never After: Rise of the Trolls*.

Something's happened.

Something terrible!

Something, she is sure, that has to do with her leaving Never After and denying the fairy mark on her forehead.

There's only one thing left to do.

She has to go back.

Chapter Twenty-Three

Never Say Never

There's no time to waste! What else could have changed in the books? Filomena decides she can't sit around waiting to find out. She's got to get back there! She has to make sure they're all still *there*. She hurriedly empties her backpack, removing her schoolbooks, and crams in as many Never After books as she can.

What if they're all gone? What if Never After is completely under the ogres' control? Why did she want to leave in the first place? She was scared, for sure. And she was worried about her parents, of course. But there was something else – something she can't admit.

It was easier to run away.

Much easier to run away than face the truth of who she is. And who is she? She'll never know if she doesn't go back.

And now, faced with the consequences of her actions, something terrible has happened. Jack is dead! What about Alistair? What's happened to him? And Zera? Did the sultan – goodness – what if the sultan killed her?

Anyway, the longer she imagines these scenarios, the more she's convinced that something terrible is happening back there. She hopes she can return some of the story to its rightful shape. Already she can see the titles of the other books changing.

Never After, Book Two: *The Ogres' Victory*

Never After, Book Seven: *The End of Westphalia*

Never After, Book Eleven: *The Reign of the Evil Queen*

It just gets worse and worse . . .

She debates telling her parents everything. Maybe it's time to be honest about what's going on. She can trust them; they're her parents. They love her no matter who – or what – she is.

Besides, she can't just leave without explaining where she's gone.

Except she can't tell them the whole truth, either: that she's off to fight a war in another world. No. That would worry them too much.

She runs downstairs and sees her parents sitting together on the couch, their legs entwined, sharing a bowl of popcorn while they watch their favourite show: *Handsome Romantic Detective*.

'Hey, honey, what's up? Where are you going?' asks Mum.

'Oh . . . ah . . . I was thinking of going to the library,' she says. She can't do it. She can't tell them.

'What for?' asks Dad.

'I was going to try to find some books about adopted kids, and adoption, you know, um, about people like me.' Playing with their guilt. Oh, she is a terrible child!

Her parents exchange worried glances, and it breaks her heart a little. Her father turns off the television. She's not allowed to walk anywhere alone, so of course her dad offers to take her there.

'It's so late,' Mum says. 'It's a school night.'

'It's OK,' Dad says, disentangling his feet from his wife's.

'Actually, I don't have to go to the library.' Filomena takes a deep breath. She's going to do it. She's going to tell them. The whole truth. Haven't her parents always assured her they'd love her no matter what? That she can tell them anything and they won't be mad?

Here goes . . .

'Mum. Dad. I know this sounds crazy, but I went to Never After. The books are real. I found out I have this!' She takes off her beanie, and the light from the crescent moon and thirteen stars shine all around the room. 'It's the mark of Carabosse. She's one of the thirteen fairies of the Great Forest. Anyway, I went there, and now I have to go back because when I left, I think it changed things. It changed the stories in the books. And now I think my friends – I have friends there, Jack and Alistair and Zera – are in danger. So I have to go through the portal again – it's in the Hollywood Hills – and you can't stop me. I have to go. I have to help them.' She takes a deep breath. She looks at her parents. She expects them to argue, to say that she's babbling. That she's caught up in those books and needs to go outside for some fresh air, maybe, and stop reading so much. (OK, they'd never say that, but something like it?)

She meets her parents' eyes for the first time since starting her rambling speech. But instead of looking shocked, her parents are looking at her thoughtfully.

Her dad stands up. 'OK, then.'

'Keys?' Mum asks.

'Got them.'

'Let's go. Betty, you coming?'

'Yes. Let me grab my coat,' her mother replies.

What's going on? Why are they taking this news so calmly?

'Well?' asks Dad. 'You said you had to go. So we'll drive you. To the Hollywood Hills, you said?'

'To the Hollywood sign,' says Filomena, mystified.

'OK, we'll take you there, come on,' says Mum. 'Pick it up, will you? You said your friends are in danger.'

'But– but– but– you believe me?' asks Filomena.

Her mother and father look at each other with just the tiniest smidge of guilt on their faces. 'It's a long story,' says Mum with a sigh.

'We'll explain when you get back,' says Dad.

'Or in the car, maybe,' says Mum. 'It's a long drive.'

'Right,' says Dad.

Filomena is flabbergasted. Were her parents abducted by fairies and replaced with changelings? These people who won't let her walk a block unchaperoned are allowing her to go somewhere that doesn't exist on any map except the kind on the very front pages of a fantasy book?

'Well, are you coming or not, darling?' asks Mum, waiting at the open door.

Filomena snaps out of her daze, and she runs to the car's back seat. She just hopes the Heart Tree portal is still there.

Prologue

The Undaunted

Carabosse would not let this ogre queen feast on her niece. Twelve fairies had given their blessing. There was only one more to give.

Hers.

And so, out of love, Carabosse cursed the princess right then and there. A dark gift to save Eliana's life. A hex to prevent impending horror and strife. A spell of misfortune to come on her sixteenth birthday – Eliana was destined to prick her finger and fall into an enchanted sleep to keep her safe from her cruel fate.

But alas, alas, all had not gone according to plan.

Eliana's betrothed, Prince Stefan, found her hidden in thorns and woke her with a kiss. The princess awoke from her enchanted sleep, and her safety was no longer her aunt's to keep.

The curse of Carabosse was broken, the gift undone.

Eliana's marriage to Prince Stefan would come next.

And, just as the thirteenth fairy had feared, Olga's fangs were then bared.

The vile queen revealed her true face, and for the flesh of her stepdaughter and step-grandchildren she had a taste.

Whom did Olga blame? When the blood was discovered and the deaths uncovered? No other than poor Prince Stefan.

The prince, she cried, the prince killed his babes and his wife! And now the prince must die! The villain blamed the saviour. The king became mad in his behaviour.

The kingdom fell to ruin.

All was lost.

. . . *Or was it?*

For Carabosse was still standing at the christening, holding the baby princess in her arms. And she had yet to cast her spell . . .

Carabosse laid the babe again in the cradle, raised her

hands to the sky and cut her palm with a dagger. As her blood dripped to the ground, she spoke in a clear and solemn voice for all of Westphalia to hear.

'This is my gift to the princess and the kingdom –

When the night falls and the moon shows its face

I curse you to thousands upon thousands of nights of sleep –

Until one carrying my mark arrives –

Until the dragons rise –

And the wolves return –

To wake you all from nightmares deep.'

Chapter Twenty-Four

The Return

Falling through the portal again is just as nauseating and gravity-defying as it was the first time. Filomena wonders if anyone ever gets used to inter-world travel. She didn't have the Pied Pipe to unlock it this time, but she did remember the melody that unlocked the heart in the tree and did a reasonable job of whistling it.

Just as before, another tree vomits her out into Never After. She looks around. Yup. She's back on the familiar hillside that looks over almost all of the kingdoms. Except this time there's a darkness in the sky, the flowers look muted and limp, and even the air around her feels tense, as if something is just about to happen. She hopes she hasn't arrived too late.

She finds the marked trail that leads to Vineland, and as she journeys back towards Zera's cottage – which she hopes is still standing – she thinks about what her parents told her on the drive to the portal.

'You see, honey, we didn't adopt you through the normal channels,' Dad began.

'Darling, we found you under a tree!' said Mum.

'A tree?'

'In a little basket.'

'There was a letter,' said Dad.

'Shoot – I forgot to grab it.'

'A letter?'

'From whoever left you there. It said that . . . well . . . it said that we had to take care of you. You were a gift to us. But that we had to keep you safe, because there were evil creatures that would come looking for you.'

'Like what kind of evil creatures?'

'Ogres, wasn't it?' asked Dad.

'Witches too. And trolls?' added Mum, tapping her chin.

'And you believed this letter?'

'Well, better safe than sorry, yes?' said Mum. 'And,

well, also if we believed what it said, it meant we could keep you. And we wanted to keep you so badly.'

So that was why. It explained their neuroses, their overprotectiveness, their suffocating, overwhelming love and fear. They'd been warned. They'd been given a task.

'Oh, and that thing on your forehead? That was on the letter too,' said Mum. 'I knew I'd seen it somewhere.'

'And you're OK with all of this?'

Dad turned round when they reached a stoplight. 'It's not a question of whether we're OK with it or not. We trust you.'

Her parents walked her all the way to the Heart Tree. Mum was trying not to cry, and Dad was frowning.

'Group hug!' said Filomena. They embraced fiercely, in a tight circle that no one wanted to break. At last, they let her go.

'Just be safe, kid, OK?' said Mum. 'We don't know where you're going or what you have to do, but know that we love you. Be brave. You are more than you seem, and you know more than you know.'

'And come back to us,' added Dad.

'I promise I will,' said Filomena fervently.

One last smile, one last hug, and she was gone.

*

She forgot that Zera's cottage is glamoured and that she isn't immune to it. Is it just through those trees, or is she standing right in front of it? It's hard to tell – everything looks so different. Many cottages are still charred from the ogre attack. Some are no longer standing. Everything in Vineland looks different, sadder, uglier and ruined. It also looks mostly deserted.

A few villagers trudge by, but no one can tell her if Jack and Alistair are still around, or where Zera's cottage is. Most of them eye her suspiciously as they hurry away.

Finally, the Cheshire Cat on his mushroom takes pity on her. 'It's over there. Right in front of you. Just knock,' the cat says, blowing a smoke ring.

She thanks him, and he gives her an enigmatic smile before disappearing.

She's standing in front of nothing, but she forces herself to knock. She raps against a solid door; she just can't see it.

She knocks again, louder this time.

From inside, someone yells, 'I'm coming, already! Hold your hairs!' just before the door swings open, revealing a stunned Alistair. 'Filomena?'

'Alistair!'

'You came back!'

'I had to!'

Alistair gives her a huge hug and doesn't let go for a while. Filomena is grateful for his kindness. 'Where's everybody?' she asks when Alistair breaks the embrace.

'Zera went to find her sisters,' says Alistair. 'But Jack's . . .'

'Here,' says Jack, who's leaning against a wall and regarding her with a cool expression on his face. 'So. The prodigal daughter returns.'

'Hey to you too,' she says, just as aloof as he is.

Alistair looks from one to the other. 'Now, now, let's not fight. Filomena's back, and that's a good thing!'

Jack shrugs as if he doesn't care either way. Filomena decides to ignore him. 'Look, I have a lot to tell you guys. First, my parents know I'm from here. There was some kind of letter from the person who left me in front of their house. It said ogres and trolls would be looking for me. Second, something went wrong with the books when I left. The story changed.'

'In what way?' asks Jack, raising an eyebrow.

'Well, um, you died,' says Filomena. 'You didn't become you.'

Alistair claps his hands over his mouth. 'I knew it!'

'What?' asks Filomena as Jack glowers.

'When you left – something happened to all of us,'

Alistair tells her. 'We all went dark.'

'Huh?'

'Popped out of existence, I think. When you left, when you rejected the mark. It's like we were never here.'

'Really?'

'Remember how I told you Never Afters can perish, but there are rules that govern our existence? But that our demise is not something we've come close to experiencing yet?'

She nods.

'Well, we've experienced it now. One day we were here, and then poof! We weren't. We just popped back right before you arrived.'

'If you guys are back, maybe the book's back too.' She removes the first volume and feels such a huge wash of relief over her. 'It's OK. Look. You're still on the cover.'

Jack finally snaps out of his gloom and picks up the book with a wry smile. 'Is that what they think I look like?'

The books are back to the original version, at least for now. Returning to Never After changed things for the better.

'Remember how I told you we're in the thirteenth book? We're all part of the story. We have to figure out how it ends,' she says.

'Happily, I hope,' quips Alistair.

'I've read all the books,' Filomena tells them. 'I think I know what to do to defeat the ogre queen and her army. We need to be prepared. We'll each need armour, a helm and weapons. Dragon's Tooth swords that can cut through anything like the one Zera had that killed the ogre general.'

'Where are we going to get all that stuff?' asks Alistair.

'The books say that the most powerful weapons are forged and made in the Deep.'

'You mean where the dragons live?' asks Jack.

'Yes.'

'Um . . .' Alistair looks reluctant.

She looks at both of them, exasperated. 'What are you guys waiting for? Let's go! We've got kingdoms to save.'

Chapter Twenty-Five

Into the Deep

'The thing is, dragons aren't one for visitors,' Jack explains. 'They keep to themselves, hoarding their gold and treasure.'

'And you know what happens to those who seek to take it from them,' adds Alistair. 'Burned to a crisp.'

'The dragons came to pay their fealty to the princess at the christening. Historically, they are supposed to be Westphalia's allies,' Filomena reminds them.

'That was in the past,' says Jack. 'It's been thousands of years, and no one has seen them since. After Carabosse cursed everyone, they kept away. And they know what's been happening up here – as Westphalia fell and the ogres took everything west of the Vale. They did nothing. They buried themselves deeper underground.'

'The Deep is way, way down below,' agrees Alistair. 'We might never find them and just get lost down there forever.'

'Don't be such a Sour Skittle,' Filomena says.

His eyebrows shoots up in confusion. 'What's a Skittle?'

'Never mind,' Filomena replies with a smile. 'When all of this is over, I'm going to bring you some candy from my world.'

Alistair lights up at this prospect. 'Candy *and* you've got to hunt me down a cheeseburger.'

'Deal,' says Filomena. 'As long as we agree to go see some dragons.'

'Well . . .' Alistair shuffles his feet while Jack remains stone-faced.

'So the alternative is just to let the ogres take over all of Never After?' Filomena crosses her arms and purses her lips. 'What happened to the guys who tricked the vizier and helped Aladdin? And rescued Alice from the Queen of Hearts?'

Alistair sighs. 'I don't know, what did happen to them? Did they stay alive, or did they get eaten by dragons?'

Jack shrugs. 'We just happened to be at the right place at the right time, that's all. We're not the heroes you think we are.'

'Yes you are, Jack Stalker,' says Filomena. 'I believe in you. These books were the best friends I ever had. Which means you guys are the best friends I've ever had.' She turns to Alistair. 'You too, Alistair.'

Alistair beams. Jack looks less reluctant.

'Come on, we have to get the dragons' help. Without it, we don't stand a chance,' says Filomena. 'And the dragons might hate visitors, but there's one thing they hate more.'

'Ogres,' say Jack and Alistair in chorus.

'You're right,' says Jack at last. 'Let's go.'

Jack brings out a map of Never After. It's similar to the ones printed in the front of the books, but more intricate, and there are trees everywhere. 'This is the portal system, where the Heart Trees lie. We need to get to the one that takes us down into the Deep.'

Filomena squints at the map. 'Looks like it's in the Dark Wood?'

'Not far,' agrees Jack.

But when they arrive at the place marked on the map, the trees are so dense and overgrown that it's difficult to ascertain which one is the portal. The forest is bathed in gloom due to the high canopy of treetops, and the deeper they walk into it, the quieter and more eerie it becomes. There are no sounds of birds or tiny woodland creatures. No squirrels run up the tree trunks; no sparrows perch on the branches. They are all alone. Every snap of a twig, every branch they brush, echoes through the woods.

'Is it just me, or are we the only ones here?' whispers Filomena.

'Everyone keeps clear of this place,' replies Alistair.

'Like I said, the dragons hate visitors,' says Jack. 'Wait. I think I found it.' He stops in front of one of the oldest trees Filomena has ever seen. Its trunk is as wide as a truck. The heart etched in its centre is a fiery one, with flames all around.

'This is it – I recognize it,' says Filomena, awed. 'It's on the cover of the tenth book.'

Jack raises an eyebrow.

'Pied Pipe?' asks Alistair, removing it from his pocket.

But Jack and Filomena shake their heads. Filomena blushes.

'Don't tell us, you read about it,' teases Jack.

'What a nerd,' Alistair says in jest, tossing her a friendly smile.

She grins at them. 'Knowledge comes in handy. You guys should try gaining some sometime.'

'OK, so how do we get in, then?' asks Alistair.

Filomena is more than happy to share. 'The dragons hate unannounced visitors. But they do like manners. So the only way into the Deep . . .'

'Is to knock,' says Jack, who does just that. He raps on the tree trunk three times.

KNOCK.

KNOCK.

KNOCK.

At last, the door to the tree opens with a creaky yawn. Beyond the doorway, through the darkness, they can see just a hint of flame.

Are they going to get cooked?

Eaten?

Dismembered?

Jack turns to his companions. 'OK, here goes. Before we go through, remember it's not all tulip cakes and Lily Licks down there. I can't tell you guys enough: do *not* joke with dragons. They have no sense of humour.'

'None?' asks Alistair with a gulp.

'None,' says Jack. 'They're the oldest creatures in

Never After. Possibly as old as the land itself, and they don't suffer fools.'

'It's fine,' says Filomena. 'We won't be one.' She shores up her courage, thinking of what her parents told her before they left: *We don't know where you're going or what you have to do, but know that we love you. Be brave. You are more than you seem, and you know more than you know.*

Jack nods and Filomena watches him walk through the gaping portal, followed by Alistair. She steels herself, closes her eyes and walks through.

And screams.

She's falling through an endless hole.

Down.

Down.

Down.

She lands with a thump in a damp, musty cavern. At least she fell on her feet this time. She looks around. 'Jack? Alistair?' she calls softly. 'Where are you guys?'

But only her voice echoes back to her.

Where are they?

What happened?

Then: the sound of heavy footsteps thundering towards her, followed by the sound of something heavy dragging behind. Its tail. Of course. A dragon. She can hear it snorting.

Filomena starts to feel hot in the cave, and she doesn't know whether it's fear or heat that's making her sweat.

At last the dragon emerges, as tall as a building, filling the entire space and breathing fire.

She stares at the magnificent creature.

And bows.

'Your Magnificence, I am Filomena Jefferson-Cho of North Pasadena, and I come to you for aid in a time of need that only the Royal Dragons of the Deep may provide.'

The dragon studies Filomena, still on her knees, bowed so low that her arms are outstretched over her head and touching the ground.

'A supplicant! We haven't had one in years. Oh, this is going to be fun.' And the dragon laughs a deep belly laugh.

Jack was wrong. Dragons do have a sense of humour – except Filomena has no idea what she just said that was so funny.

Chapter Twenty-Six

The Show of Strength

All in all, it wasn't too bad, thought Alistair. At least the dragon didn't eat them *right away*. No, like all those higher up the food chain, dragons liked to play with their dinner first. And they are definitely dragon dinner.

These dragons hadn't eaten in a long time.

The one who found him was practically salivating. 'Yer a little one, but ye'll do,' said the dragon.

The three of them had fallen in different places in the Deep, but each had been caught by a dragon and placed in some kind of holding cell overlooking a vast cavern. At least they were all together.

Filomena is a little spooked, Jack weary and Alistair – well, to be honest, he is just one moment away from COMPLETELY FREAKING OUT. But he is holding it in. This is worse than just popping out of existence for a moment and then popping back. That experience was odd. This one is just spine-chilling. Is it terrible that he doesn't want to be eaten? That's a reasonable goal, isn't it?

The dragon – the one who brought Filomena – comes back and regards the three of them thoughtfully.

'Supplicants to the Deep, your presence is uninvited and undesired; however, it is not unappreciated. You raise the old treaty between the Deep and Above, between dragon and fairy. Our council has decided to honour that treaty.'

Yay! mouths Alistair.

Jack kicks him in the shin. 'Shhhh.'

The dragon looks annoyed to have been interrupted and snorts a plume of smoke in their faces.

'We shall provide aid that can only be provided by the Deep. However: you must earn our protection and assistance by proving your worth in a Game of Threes.'

'How convenient, since there are three of us,' Alistair mutters.

Jack kicks him again.

The dragon pretends not to have noticed this time. 'Each of you must pass your challenge, or help is forfeit, as are your lives. The Deep shall take its due.'

The dragon disappears, leaving them alone in the darkness once more.

'The Game of Threes, the Game of Threes,' says Filomena. 'I can't remember – but I feel like it has to be in the books somewhere. I just don't remember how to win.' She's fretting and tearing through the books she has in her backpack. 'I should have brought all twelve of them, but they were so heavy.'

'There's no way,' says Alistair. 'We're dinner. I hope I'm tasty.'

Jack walks over to Filomena and steadies her hand, closing the book. 'The answer's not in there. Don't worry. It's a game. Which means there's a way to win. There's *always* a way to win. That's why it's called a game. Dragons hate cheaters more than they hate visitors. They won't cheat. We can win fair and square, get them to help us and get out of here.'

'Oh,' says Filomena, looking at Jack with clear admiration.

'You can do this, Alistair,' says Jack. 'You can win.'

Alistair gulps. It was so easy to believe in his friends,

so much harder to believe in himself.

When the dragon returns, he nods at Alistair.

'Me?' he squeaks.

'Alistair Bartholomew Barnaby,' says the dragon. 'You have been chosen to perform the Show of Strength.'

'Me?' Alistair squeaks again. He wonders how the dragon knew his name, but then dragons know many things.

'Come,' the dragon orders.

'Good luck,' whispers Filomena.

'Remember, there is always a way to win,' says Jack, holding out a fist as he'd seen the mortals do.

Alistair pounds it. 'Right.'

Alistair follows the dragon out towards the open arena floor. He's trying to be brave, but he's never been brave. That's the whole point of being Jack Stalker's best friend: You didn't have to be brave or courageous or fearless; you can just hide behind Jack. That's what Alistair is good at, hiding. Why is there nowhere to hide right now? And why was he picked first? He put up a brave front for Jack and Filomena, but in reality, he is terrified.

They're in the arena now, and he can see Jack and Filomena up at the cave where they are imprisoned.

They're craning their necks and looking down to see him. Jack waves, and Filomena gives a thumbs-up.

The rocky arena is completely empty, and the dragon flies away to the other end, where three dragons are sitting on dragon thrones. They must be the council.

'The test of strength shall now begin!' a voice booms from overhead. 'We wish you bad luck and ill fortune. However, if you pass the Show of Strength, you will be one step closer to earning our munificence and your lives back.'

Alistair quakes in his boots.

The ground beneath him rumbles and, to Alistair's horror, the very earth breaks open and a row of sharp stalagmites rises up from the cavern floor like puncturing spikes in varying size and thickness. Behind him rises a cage holding an angry-looking dragon. The dragon spies Alistair and releases a howl of fire and rage.

Alistair screams and steps back, almost tripping over a stalagmite. It's clear he has to make his way past the spikes to get away from the dragon, whose cage slowly begins to open.

He turns back to the sharp rocks. Is he supposed to budge them? How? They're thousands of years old. He was chosen for this because he's weak, he knows. Then he stops himself. Sure, he's not as brave as Jack or as smart as Filomena, but neither of them is gifted with strength, either. Maybe he's not as weak as he thinks.

Think, Alistair, think.

He keeps pushing at the rocks. Nothing.

What can he do?

Behind him, he can hear the cage door creaking slowly as it opens. But he can't give in to the fear. The fear will blind him. He can't give in to the fear. He has to focus.

Maybe if he kicks them? He kicks one of the smaller stalagmites, to no avail. His frustration is growing. He looks at the obstacle, side to side, in its entirety. He tries to climb through the stalagmites, but there are too many, and his shirt snags on one and tears. There's no way this is going to work.

He moves from column to column, pulling and pushing and trying to break or shift the obstacles.

The caged dragon hisses and lets out a blazing breath, the flames licking the walls around them.

Alistair screams again, covering his head. But he's still in one piece. He's got to think! He's got to figure this out! Then he hears Jack's voice in his head: *It's a game . . . There's always a way to win.*

Then he sees it: a boulder. A round boulder. And

when he looks at the row of stalagmites, he's reminded of something he saw in the mortal world. A game they played, in the building where there were bins outside full of – what did Filomena call it? Trash pizza.

Inside, the mortals rolled the ball towards standing pins of some sort, and the pins crashed. It was a game. The pins looked a lot like the spikes in front of him now.

Alistair races for the boulder, hoping against all odds that he's able to lift it, or at least roll it. He's out of breath, panting and wheezing, as he runs. He grabs the boulder and calculates that if he can roll it from a slight incline in the arena, it will have more momentum and the strength to crash through the spikes. Determination gives him the last bit of strength he needs as he pushes the rock up the slope.

With one last grunt, he shoves the boulder as hard as he can from the top of the incline, sending it rolling down towards the stalagmites. It picks up speed as it rolls, hurtling into the middle of the spikes.

With a crashing sound, the first bunch of stalagmites breaks apart and falls.

Alistair hears his friends cheering him on as he races towards the spikes to grab the boulder among the rubble and then begins to roll it back up the slight hill to start over again. He sends it plummeting downhill towards the stalagmites, aiming for the same spot where he'd knocked down the first grouping.

The boulder rolls towards the spikes, picking up pace once more as it heads straight for his intended target, and it knocks down several more stalagmites. The crumbling columns crash down into rubble, and light emerges from where they'd just been blocking the path.

The dragon roars in frustration as Alistair runs through the path and out of the arena to safety.

When he looks back, the dragon's cage door shuts with a bang.

Alistair swings his fist in the air triumphantly.

'Congratulations,' hisses a booming voice, just as Filomena and Jack pop out of the tunnel and run to hug Alistair.

'Oh my ogre! I did it! I really did it!' he yells.

'You did!' says Filomena. 'You really did!'

Jack thumps him on his back. 'I knew you would!'

The booming voice bellows again, clearly unmoved. 'You may go on to the next challenge. Please make your way through the path to see what danger lies ahead.'

And, just like that, their relief morphs back into fear as

they realize they still have two challenges left to determine their survival. They step over the stalagmite rubble and head to the next part of the game, with danger lapping at their backs.

Chapter Twenty-Seven

Test of Wills

The second arena is covered in flames from the bottom of the cave floor all the way to the top of the cavern. The heat has settled into their surroundings, filling the cave with an uncomfortable warmth and intensity that instantly makes them sweat. Jack looks away. Somehow he knows this is his challenge.

'The second challenge is the Test of Wills,' says the voice. 'We have chosen Jack the Giant Stalker toface it.'

He knew it.

'No magic is allowed. To move on to the next and final

test, you must walk through the flames to the other side. Begin.'

'Jack!' says Filomena.

He turns to her. She's frantic. 'In the books – the Test of Wills is not only about willpower but about mind power. If you can recognize the unreal for what it is, you can succeed. If you can put your mind over the mischief in front of you, you can manage. It's not real. It's just a test of your mind and your will to survive.'

'You will. Survive, I mean,' says Alistair with a cheer-up grin. 'You're Jack Stalker.'

Before Jack can thank them, Filomena and Alistair disappear from his side with a *whoosh*. When he looks up, he sees them in a cavern not unlike the one in which he and Filomena watched Alistair.

His stomach twists, and his eyes water. For he knows his friends are going to watch him burn. Because he can't do this.

Jack gazes into the fire.

He's Jack the Giant Stalker. The boy who bested the giant. What did Filomena call him? The 'dashing hero' of the story. But it's not true. He's no hero. Not when he was needed most.

When he looks into the growing inferno, all he

can see is the way the fire danced over his village, destroying everything in its path. He was coming back from the giant's feast when he saw it: the shack his family lived in, covered in flames. He heard their screams. He ran towards the blaze. He made it inside the house.

There was smoke everywhere, and he couldn't see.

Then he heard it, the sickening crash of the roof.

He had to run out before he was killed.

The screams stopped.

They were dead. His mother, his brother. It had been just the three of them, and now it was just Jack.

He was burning He hadn't realized until villagers pushed him down, rolled him and put out the flames. At first he wouldn't let the pixies heal him. He wanted to remember the pain of that moment.

Even though his scars have healed, he will never forget. He looks down at the vines covering his arms. They're in stasis; they can't help him now. No magic is allowed, and no magic will work in this arena. This is just him and the fire.

Jack wills his feet to move.

But he can't.

Move, he says to himself, grimacing. *Move*.

The flames dance closer.

If he doesn't move, the fire will move to him.

He takes one small step forward. He's covered in sweat, dripping from his forehead to his nose.

His home, burning. His mother's screams. His brother's pain.

He walks into the fire, the flaming path before him burning a mixture of bright oranges, yellows, and reds. It engulfs him; he can feel it, his face, his hair, his body. He's burning.

No!

He isn't.

It's a test.

A test of will.

He can believe he's burning, or he can – what did Filomena say? – put his mind above the mischief and he will succeed.

With enormous effort, Jack pushes aside the past, the memories that have haunted him for years. He drowns out the screams and replaces them with silence. He focuses on walking forward, ignoring the burning of his hands, the fire that is all around him.

He couldn't save his family. But he can save his friends.

He can do this.

He keeps walking although he can no longer feel his feet.

And at last he is through.

The flames are behind him.

He looks at his hands. They are the same, unburnt. He is whole. He collapses when he reaches the other end of the arena.

But his friends are there to catch him.

Filomena is crying. Alistair looks like a ghost.

'You did it,' she whispers.

'Badass,' says Alistair. 'I learned that in the mortal world.' He asks Filomena, 'That's right, isn't it?'

She smiles. 'Totally.'

The booming voice returns. 'Congratulations. You have made it to the third and final challenge. Filomena Jefferson-Cho of North Pasadena, you must pass this test or fail your quest. Continue to the next arena.'

Chapter Twenty-Eight

The Riddle

It's her turn. After Jack has bested the dragons in the Test of Wills, which challenged his bravery and determination, and Alistair has shown that strength can come from ingenuity and observation, it's now her turn to face the dragons. Jack and Alistair are walking down the path to the next arena, Jack limping a little, when they notice she's not with them.

Alistair turns around. Filomena hasn't moved an inch.

She knows what this looks like, how much of a coward she is, but she can't seem to make her legs move forward.

'Fil?' Alistair asks gently. 'It's OK.'

She shakes her head and chokes back a sob. 'I don't know if I can do this. I'll never forgive myself if I let you guys down.'

Alistair smiles. 'Well, that's the thing. If you fail, you won't have to forgive yourself. We'll all be dragon dinner.'

Even Jack chuckles at that. He edges his way over. The challenge took a lot out of him, and he's still not quite himself. 'What are you scared of?' he asks.

Filomena shrugs. 'Everything. Everything depends on me right now, and I've never been good under pressure. I know you won't understand, but I'm not the kind of person who "tests well". What if I don't make it? What if I fail?' she whispers. This isn't like a C-minus in algebra. If she doesn't pass the challenge, she will doom them to death. Her earlier bravado – storming out of the house, telling her parents the truth, shaking Jack and Alistair up and forcing them to travel to the Deep – it's all left her.

She's absolutely terrified. Frozen.

Jack seems to have recovered his cool, and he looks at her sternly. 'Then at least you've tried. The quickest way to fail is to succumb to your doubt and fear. If you never try, you'll never know if you could have succeeded, which makes it *certain* that you'll fail.'

'You've got to try,' says Alistair. 'You can do it. I believe in you.'

'We believe in you,' agrees Jack. It might be the nicest thing anyone besides her parents has ever said to her.

Her parents!

Filomena remembers what they said to her. *Be brave. You are more than you seem, and you know more than you know. Come back to us.*

'Now, come along,' Alistair says soothingly. 'The last challenge awaits. You're smart. You're a reader. Maybe you even know what's about to happen. If anyone can do this, it's you.'

Jack nods.

'Come on,' says Jack, looping an arm through hers while Alistair takes the other side. Together, the three of them march towards their fate.

The next arena is neither covered with spikes nor covered in flame. The space is dark and empty and, once more, the two who are not part of the challenge are soon sent to observe from a crevice high above the cavern floor.

Filomena stands alone in the centre of the arena.

'Filomena Jefferson-Cho, it is time for the third challenge. The Riddle. True wit is unknown to the earthly. Three cries for your inevitable demise,' booms the invisible voice.

She grits her teeth and glares at the void. They dragons are rooting for her to fail. They want her to stumble. They will celebrate her downfall. And now, in this moment, all she wants is to prove them wrong.

'Listen closely,' the voice commands. 'I am small but stand tall. I can rise but I can fall. I am light, I am flight, in the day or in the night. With the wind I can dance, on the ground I stand no chance. As one I am none but with more I may soar. Wet I can float, dry I can fly. I may not cry, but I may lie. If you are you, what am I?'

Filomena's brow wrinkles in response as she thinks.

Why does the riddle sound familiar? Almost as if she's heard it before.

Maybe you've read this one before, Alistair said. *You always seem to know what happens here.*

She goes over the riddle line by line. *I am small but stand tall.* Something tiny?

I can rise but I can fall. A person?

I am light, I am flight, in the day or in the night. The sun?

I may not cry, but I can lie.

Nothing makes sense – but it's a riddle. A word game. Wordplay. Words can have lots of meanings. 'I am light' does not have to mean light as in sunlight or daylight; it can mean something that's not heavy. 'I may not cry' means it's not a person or an animal but an object. 'I can lie' means that whatever it is can be set down.

It's coming to her.

It's almost there.

She can picture it.

But why is it so familiar?

She goes over the riddle again.

With the wind I can dance, on the ground I stand no chance. As one I am none but with more I may soar. Wet I can float, dry I can fly.

What soars and flies?

A bird?

She almost has it.

She glances up to where Jack and Alistair are watching. Alistair is gnawing on his fingernails, while Jack has the same cool, collected demeanour he always has. The quiet in the arena is so loud that she can hear her heart beating. It feels like time is moving in slow motion, like the whole world is waiting on her. Waiting on her to guess. Waiting on her to answer. Waiting on her to save their kingdom.

Filomena closes her eyes, picturing the words in her mind. *Wait a minute*, she thinks. *The reason this sounds so familiar . . . is because I wrote it.*

She can see the inky handwriting on the page. Words and phrases crossed out. But when did she do this?

Filomena squares her shoulders and speaks in a voice that echoes and carries all over the arena. 'I am small but stand tall. I can rise but I can fall. I am light, I am flight, in the day or in the night. With the wind I can dance, on the ground I stand no chance. As one I am none but with more I may soar. Wet I can float, dry I can fly. I may not cry, but I may lie. If you are you, what am I?' she asks. And she answers, 'A feather.'

There is a loud hiss of annoyance before the booming voice acknowledges her victory. 'A feather it is. You have bested us in the Game of Threes. Your petition will be heard by the council. Proceed to the royal court.'

Alistair and Jack suddenly appear in the centre of the arena and run over to her, impressed and buoyant. But as much as she wishes she could genuinely take part in rejoicing with them, she can't.

Because Filomena is not only stunned but baffled. She knows she wrote that riddle, but she cannot remember *when* – or why. Winning a challenge of wit by answering a riddle she herself wrote may technically constitute cheating (if anyone is being technical), but it's not really cheating unless you *knowingly* do something wrong.

It's not her fault they asked her the very same riddle she came up with herself. Only . . . when and *why*, exactly, did she write it?

But there's no more time to puzzle over that question. They are being ushered to plead their case in front of the Royal Dragons of the Deep.

Chapter Twenty-Nine

Fire and Blood

They follow their dragon guide to yet another cavern, but this one isn't dark like the earlier ones. This one is practically blazing with light, and when they get closer, Filomena realizes it's because there is so much gold piled inside the cave. It's hard to look at the three dragons who are sitting on the hoard.

These dragons who assess them are so large that they make the dragon who led them here look like a pony. They're easily as tall as skyscrapers, and old . . . so old.

'Who dares wake us from our sleep?' grumbles the one on the right.

'Supplicants! We haven't seen a supplicant who's survived our game in centuries,' rasps the dragon on the left.

The one in the middle is the largest. That dragon turns a large, wizened serpent face towards them. 'I am Darius, keeper of the Deep. To my left is Maximus, and to my right is Saleyeth.'

Filomena curtsies. 'Filomena Jefferson-Cho of North Pasadena.'

'Jack Stalker the Giant Slayer. Pleased to make your acquaintance,' Jack says.

'Alistair Bartholomew Barnaby. I like your dragon bed,' Alistair offers innocently. 'What's it made of?'

'Gold, and the bones of our enemies,' Darius replies grimly.

'Ew,' Alistair says without thinking.

Darius tilts his head in challenge, silently daring Alistair to speak ill of the lair again, and this time it's Filomena who kicks his shin.

'Ow!' Alistair yelps.

'Please forgive our friend for his lack of manners,' says Jack.

Darius seems willing to let it go. 'For thousands upon thousands of nights, we have slept in the Deep, untroubled by the world Above. What do you seek from the Deep? Your valour has won you an audience, nothing more. But speak freely and we may consider your request.'

Once again Filomena bows low. 'Your Eminences, the lands above you are in danger of falling to the ogre queen who seeks to destroy us all. Things are dire, and every day one more kingdom falls to her power. We must fight, but we cannot do so without the armour and weapons forged in the Deep.'

'She speaks the truth, Your Greatnesses,' says Jack. 'We need your help if we are to save Never After from this danger.'

'The affairs above are of no concern to us,' says Saleyeth, a beautiful golden female dragon. 'No one has ever cared for dragons' welfare. Why should we lift a claw in anyone's favour?'

'The ogre queen will not be satisfied until she has all of Never After under her command,' Jack warns. 'Once she's conquered all the kingdoms Above, she will look for more lands to conquer. She will come down here, seeking gold and riches.'

'Let her come,' says Saleyeth angrily. 'We will show her what happens to thieves.'

'Please, Your Eminences!' cries Filomena. 'Once upon a time you came to Westphalia to celebrate the birth of its princess! You promised to honour the alliance between Above and Below. We need your help desperately.'

Darius swishes his tail, and the gold beneath him clinks. 'We did send emissaries. It seemed a fortunate boon. But that was thousands of years ago.'

'Merely a blink of a dragon's eye,' says Filomena.

Darius smiles, showing his sharp fangs.

'Please,' says Alistair simply. 'Please help us.'

The three dragons exchange suspicious looks, and Maximus breathes fire unexpectedly, letting out a low growl 'And *how* exactly do three small children plan to defeat the ogre queen and her army? Do *you* have an army of your own behind you?'

'Well, no . . . ' says Alistair.

'Not exactly . . . ' Filomena replies. 'Well, not just yet, anyway. But we will. Once we can get the remaining fairies together . . .'

The dragons laugh, deeply and savagely, causing the entire room to shake.

'It's not funny!' Filomena cries. In the heat of the moment, she removes her beanie, and the radiant mark of the thirteenth fairy glows in the dimly lit room, catching the dragons' attention.

Darius rises to his monstrous feet and stomps slowly to

Filomena, bending down to inspect the mark on her forehead.

'Is it real?' Salayeth enquires.

Darius lets out a monstrous huff, like he's thinking, and the sudden blow of air sends Filomena's hair flying back as she squints. 'It appears so,' Darius finally responds.

'It is real,' Jack confirms. 'It is the mark of Carabosse.'

'Carabosse,' says Maximus approvingly. 'Now, she was a fairy.'

'Carabosse was a friend to the Deep,' says Darius with a frown. 'We are pledged to help any who carry her mark.'

'But Carabosse was magnificent, and this one is so . . . *small*,' Maximus responds indignantly.

'A speck,' agrees Saleyeth, gazing at her claws. 'Not even worth a chomp.'

'I'm glad I'm . . . unappetizing,' says Filomena.

Darius seems to have made up his mind and speaks for the three. 'Small as she is, she is marked by our friend. And we dragons are loyal above all. We will aid you in your battle against the ogres. With one condition: the treaty between Deep and Above is that we stay to our spaces. But I find we are weary of the darkness. We wish to fly in the sun once more. If we help you defeat the ogre queen, we must be allowed back in Westphalia. We will not be hunted, nor shall we hunt in return.'

'Your Eminence, your generosity is beyond imagination,' says Filomena. 'But please let us talk about it before we accept.'

The dragons huff. Then Darius flicks his claw and Filomena, Jack and Alistair find themselves alone in a cave outside the royal cavern.

'Can we give them what they want?' asks Filomena.

'Technically, no, since we're not the royal family of Westphalia.'

'But the royal family is missing.'

'So maybe we can pledge on their behalf?' asks Alistair. 'What could it hurt?'

'They'll kill us if they think they've been deceived,' says Jack.

'But we don't have a choice.'

'How do we know they won't turn round and slaughter everyone in Westphalia once the ogres are defeated?' he asks.

'We'll just have to trust them,' says Filomena.

'Yikes,' says Alistair.

'They'll keep their word. I know they will,' she says.

Jack sighs. 'All right.'

As if the dragons know the trio is done, the supplicants are popped back in front of the royal council.

'On behalf of the royal family of Westphalia, we accept the terms of your agreement,' says Filomena.

Darius, in lieu of answering with words, begins to wriggle and groan, almost as if in pain. Slowly and painstakingly, he sheds the scales on his left claw, like a glove that's become too large for him. It rests at his feet, sharp and shiny. 'You have my word. To seal that word as true, as a promise to be honoured until the end of time, we will give you our scales as armour for your army.'

Jack reaches down to touch the dragonhide. It's unexpectedly light, like woven threads of gold and silver.

'These scales have endured for millennia. May they protect you and yours for the rest of your time.'

The other two dragons rise, repeating the act, with Maximus offering his scales to Alistair, and Salayeth offering hers to Filomena.

'As for weaponry . . .' Darius rummages through the pile of treasure underneath him and removes a wrapped bundle, laying it in front of them. He uncloaks it, revealing a set of fangs in different sizes and shapes, forged into swords and daggers.

'Whoa!' Alistair exclaims, leaning forward to stare at the gift. Then he looks up at Darius, asking, 'Are those what I think they are?'

The dragon nods. 'Dragon's Teeth are known for both their deadly and mystical properties. They are as protective as they are perilous. For centuries, they have been used to penetrate even the thickest and most spellbound armour, aiding in some of the most crucial battles of all time.'

'Is it true that even just the sight of a Dragon's Tooth can paralyse an opponent with fear?' Filomena asks.

Darius pauses, considering the question. 'That answer depends on how powerful the particular opponent is, as well as what kind of magic or sorcery the enemy wields against you.'

Alistair and Jack pause at that, eyeing Filomena, as though they're thinking the same thing she is: *What will the ogre queen have in her arsenal?*

Darius wraps the bundle back up and hands it to Jack. 'May these weapons protect and defend your cause. You carry the blessings of the Deep in your battle.'

'Defeat the ogres,' orders Salayeth. 'I long to see the sun once more.'

'Blessings upon you three,' adds Maximus. 'May you bring peace and glory back to Westphalia.'

Filomena, Jack and Alistair bow low to the dragons and thank them for their gifts.

'One last thing,' says Darius, before bidding the trio

farewell and letting them back through the portal to Vineland. 'You were wise to seek the power of the Deep. But that is not enough. All of Westphalia must stand against the ogre witch if the kingdom is to survive. And if soldiers are what you are looking for, look no further than the Wolves of the Wood.'

Chapter Thirty

Tinker, Tailor, Cobbler, Fashion Designer

'What do we do now?' asks Alistair, his dragon scales draped over his shoulder as the three friends trudge through the woods back to the cottage. 'Look for the wolves?'

'Not yet,' says Filomena. 'We've got to get this stuff made into armour first. We've got to find the Tailor.' She tells them that in the book series, the Tailor is conscripted by a prince to create the most durable armour from a bolt of dragonhide. 'In the books it says he plies his trade on StarWalk.'

'StarWalk?' Jack shakes his head. 'Never heard of it.'

'Rumour has it the Tailor went through the portal and never returned,' says Alistair.

'Portal to where?' asks Filomena.

'The mortal world,' says Alistair. 'Isn't that right?'

Jack nods. 'When the ogres began their rampages, a few of those in our world thought it would be safer on the mortal side.'

'StarWalk,' Filomena repeats. 'I *know* I know that place.'

'Because you read about it?' says Alistair.

'Yes. But . . . not just in the books.' She puts her hands on her hips. 'Back in Hollywood, there's something called the Walk of Fame, with a bunch of stars on the sidewalk. It's also called the Walk of Stars. StarWalk. Could that be it?'

'A walk made of stars? And I thought there was no magic in the mortal world,' says Alistair, a bit awed.

'No, they're, like, made of concrete,' she explains. 'Stone.' But her mind is racing. If StarWalk is in the books and the mortal world, is it possible that part of the story of Never After is set in her world?

After they pass through the portal and get to Hollywood Boulevard, Filomena shows them the StarWalk.

Alistair begins reading the names carved on the ground. 'Who are they?'

'They're stars for the stars. It's an award of sorts, in recognition of a person's success and talent,' Filomena says. 'Mostly they're celebrities.'

'Celebrities?'

'They're the famous people of this world. They're mostly actors, singers, musicians. "Stars", we call them. Like . . . instead of the stars we look up to in the sky, they're the people we look up to.'

Jack raises an eyebrow, finding this odd. 'Why would you look up to other people instead of stars?'

Filomena laughs. 'You have a point.'

Alistair, bored with their conversation, begins to hop from star to star.

'Stop that! You look like a tourist,' says Filomena, slightly mortified.

'What's a tourist?'

'Someone who's not from here . . . Oh yeah . . .'

Alistair shoots her a smug smile.

Filomena checks in the book and looks up at the street signs. '*Follow the path of the stars, across Vine to find the Cobbler's tailor shop.*' She glances up at a shabby storefront. 'I think this is it.'

'You think?'

'I'm sure,' she says. 'This is my wheelhouse.'

'Wheelhouse?' Jack repeats.

'I think she means one of those things,' says Alistair, pointing at a car passing by.

Filomena shakes her head. 'That's definitely not what I mean. Forget it. Just follow me.'

A bell tinkles as they step inside the shop, which is filled with bolts of fabric and mannequins, as well as shoes and boots in various degrees of repair, but no sign of a tailor or clerk.

On the wall behind the counter is a vintage black-and-white photograph of a genial older man wearing spectacles and smiling underneath a thick moustache, with a tape measure around his neck.

Jack studies the picture carefully. 'That's the Cobbler, all right.'

'Cobbler? I thought he was the Tailor,' says Alistair.

'He's both,' says Filomena. '*Mr Cobbler, the Tailor,*' she says, reading from the book.

'Ahem,' says a voice, and a short person who can only be described as an elf enters from the back room. 'Can I help you?' he greets them. Then he recognizes Jack and Alistair and begins to jump up and down. 'Jack! Alistair!'

233

'Bumple?' asks Jack.

'Yeah, how long has it been, man?' says the elf.

'Too long.'

'Hey, B,' says Alistair. 'This is Filomena.'

'You guys moving here too?' asks Bumple. 'That bad back in the NA, huh?'

'Nah, we just have to talk to your boss,' says Alistair.

'Mr C?'

'Yeah, we've got some dragonhide for him to turn into armour,' says Jack, motioning to the rolled-up bundle under his arm.

'Dragonhide? You don't say. All right, come in the back with me.'

At the back is the tailor's workshop, occupied by working elves. One elf is on a ladder, reaching for material, while another is on the floor, stitching shoes together, and the last is seated at the desk. All three of the elves seem like they work too many hours on too little sleep.

Jack unrolls the three bundles on the nearest worktable.

Bumple surveys the shimmering gold-and-silver dragonhide with admiration. 'You got this from the Deep?' He whistles.

The other elves gather around, studying the dragonhide and gently touching it with the edges of their fingers. One takes out a magnifying glass, examining the dragonhide for authenticity. 'It's real dragonhide, all right,' he says.

'We need it made into armour,' says Jack. 'Can you guys handle that?'

'Yeah, here's the thing. Mr C retired a long time ago. He moved to Boca a few years back,' says Bumple, who's smoothing down the scales.

'Boca?' asks Alistair.

'It's a place where, um, old people go,' says Filomena. 'Where it's always warm.'

'Isn't it warm here?' asks Alistair.

'You have a point,' says Filomena.

'He's really gone?' asks Jack.

Bumple and the elves nod. 'Years ago,' says Bumple. 'Sometimes he sends postcards, though.'

The three look crestfallen.

'But don't fret,' the elf adds. 'His daughter, Gretel, runs the business now. She might be able to help you guys out. Crumple, go get Miss G.'

The smallest elf disappears through another back door, and a few minutes later they meet Miss Gretel Cobbler.

They hear her before they see her: a sweet but slightly high-pitched voice that rings with too much enthusiasm to squeeze into one young lady. Like her father in the photo, Gretel has a tape measure round her neck, but hers is hot pink. She's also wearing a smile (but no moustache).

'Crumple said you guys needed me?' asks Gretel, who looks to be about thirteen and looks as if she might be one of the 'stars' in the mortal world, with glossy, styled hair and eye-catching jewellery.

Introductions are made all around. 'Jack Stalker!' says Gretel as she greets them. 'Hang on, you're Jill's brother!'

Jack smiles. 'Cousin.'

'Cousin? I thought you were twins,' says Gretel. 'Huh.'

'Everyone always assumes, since we look alike, but we're not,' says Jack. 'After our village was raided, Jill left for the beach, and now she sells seashells by the seashore.'

'Cool beans,' says Gretel. She welcomes Filomena and Alistair and then spies the scales on the worktable.

'Whoa! Is that dragonhide?' she squeals, reaching for the material. Her eyes shine. 'I've never actually even met a dragon. Daddy took us back to where he's from once, but then he lost us in the woods and some ogre witch tried to, um, eat me and my brother, and we've been here ever since, for our safety.' She runs her hands over the scales reverently.

'Wasn't that scary?' asks Alistair.

'Sort of, but, hey, after almost being put in an oven himself, Hansel's a really famous baker now,' says Gretel. 'So it wasn't all bad.' She points to another photograph on the wall, of a proud lad who looks a little like Gretel – he has the same cheerful smile – standing before a storefront that reads HANSEL'S CAKES.

Gretel thrums her fingers along her chin. 'I've never worked with dragonhide before.' Then her voice hushes as she takes Filomena by the arm and leads her to rack of beautiful and intricately made dresses. 'Are you sure it has to be a suit?'

'Yes, like a suit of armour,' replies Filomena.

'Hmm, I was thinking more like a ball gown!' Gretel exclaims.

'Suit. Armour. Like for a knight,' Filomena elaborates. 'For battle.'

Gretel puts her hands on her hips. 'But just because it's ready-for-battle-wear doesn't mean it can't be on trend, right?'

Filomena shakes her head vehemently.

'Plus, they say if you *look* good, you feel good. Don't you want to head off into war feeling proud and confident?' wheedles Gretel.

'I guess?' says Filomena, who's not so sure.

'Trust me!' says Gretel. 'I've got this!'

'Fine, Gretel. But, please, no pink, OK?'

Gretel's face lights up with a smile. 'Deal!'

Filomena sighs. She just hopes there are no rhinestones. She will *not* be the laughing-stock of the entire battlefield.

Chapter Thirty-One

There and Back Again

Gretel tells the three friends that it'll take thenight to get the suits of armour made from the dragonhide and, as a bonus, the workshop will fashion sheaths for the Dragon's Teeth as well. 'Elves work best when everyone is asleep,' she says with a wink. 'Everything will be ready by morning. Come back then!'

For a moment, Filomena, Jack and Alistair look uncomfortable; they have nowhere to stay for the night. Filomena has ruled out going home – it would be too much to see her parents only to have to leave them again. They're chill but not *that* chill. They're going to want her to stay home this time, she's sure.

When Gretel realizes they have nowhere to go, she invites them to stay at her place, above the workshop. She even makes them dinner, after asking if they're allergic to anything. Jack and Alistair don't understand her question.

'Like, if you can't eat anything cos it might give you a rash or something? Or if you're gluten-free, so you can't eat bread?' Filomena tries to explain.

'I would starve if I couldn't eat bread,' says Alistair, mystified.

'No, no allergies. Anything is fine. Even trash pizza,' says Jack.

Gretel laughs and says no one's eating from the garbage and everyone has to get washed up. It's the first time they realize they're all dirty and dishevelled from the trip to the Deep, and no one has had a bath in a while. After refreshing themselves, her friends proclaim that the shower is 'magic' and Alistair uses almost all the hot water. Gretel gives them robes and puts their dirty clothes in the washer and dryer. Soon everyone is as clean and shiny as Gretel's kitchen.

'I've made pasties and pot pie,' she announces, taking something sweet-smelling, crusty and bubbling out of the oven.

'I wish my mother could cook,' says Filomena, sitting

on a counter stool and watching with admiration. 'But all we ever do is order takeout.'

'It's easy,' says Gretel. 'I'll teach you one day. My brother taught me.'

While they tuck into the meal, they tell Gretel why they need the armour so badly. About the war between the fairies and the ogres, and how the ogres are winning.

She looks at the three of them sternly. 'So, let me get this straight: You three are going back there again to . . . battle an evil witch?'

'And her ogre armies,' says Filomena.

'Is that safe?' asks Gretel

'Oh no, not at all,' says Alistair cheerfully.

Gretel looks concerned. 'Should I pack you guys a lunch or something?'

'Sure! Cheeseburgers!' says Alistair.

The next morning, Gretel has left them breakfast on the kitchen counter – Hansel's muffins – and after eating they walk down to the shop. Gretel has already suited up the armour on three mannequins, and when she greets them, they notice she's wearing one of the suits of armour as well. 'Oh!' she says. 'There was a ton of extra dragonhide, so I made a bunch more and thought I'd try one on.' She's designed the armour so that it looks like a sleek, modern wet suit, except made from gold-and-silver scales.

'Keep it,' says Filomena.

'Truly?' asks Gretel. 'I've never had anything like this. And you're right – it's better than a ball gown.'

'It's yours,' says Filomena, giving her a hug.

Gretel laughs in delight.

The rest of them take theirs into the dressing rooms to change. Jack and Alistair put their armour on underneath their tunics, trousers and cloaks, so they look the same as before, except their arms are covered in the gold-and-silver scales. Jack's vines peep out of the hem. Filomena puts on her usual hoodie and jeans over her armour. There. Much better. She slides her Dragon's Tooth into its sheath, holstered on her hip. Now they're ready to face the ogre queen and her army.

Gretel looks a bit wistful as they say goodbye.

'Come with us!' says Alistair.

'Me?'

'Yes!' says Filomena. 'Come with. You already have the armour on too!'

'But Daddy says it's dangerous,' says Gretel.

'Well, it is,' says Jack. 'He's not wrong. Ogres on the march, war everywhere.'

'Which means we need all the help we can get,' says Filomena.

Gretel looks doubtful. 'I have always wanted to go back . . .'

The dragons warned they would need many on their side if they were to defeat the ogres. Filomena presses their case. 'Then come with us.'

Gretel sighs. 'Well, Daddy is in Boca for the winter. What he doesn't know won't hurt him. And there aren't any princes around here. Not that I need one, of course, but a girl can't help wanting to look.'

'So many princes in Never After,' says Filomena. 'Right, guys?'

Alistair and Jack shrug, utterly confounded by the conversation.

'But, remember, this isn't a matchmaking mission. It's a dangerous war,' Filomena tells Gretel.

'Explosions, fire, weapons and all that,' says Alistair. 'And lots of flesh-eating ogres. So. Many. Ogres.'

'That means I should put my hair in a bun, yes?' is all Gretel says as she pulls her hair up and looks at herself critically in the mirror. 'I don't need a blow-dry for the battlefield. But if I'm going to Never After I will need to pack.'

However, when they get to the Heart Tree portal, they discover that the formerly large and majestic oak tree is nothing but a stump.

'Oh dear!' cries Alistair. 'The tree! The poor tree!'

Jack is angry, and his vines are slithering and twitching as if looking for something to strangle. 'Whoever did this will pay.'

'Someone knows we're here,' says Filomena. 'And someone doesn't want us to go back.' She thinks of the Ogre's Wrath that followed them last time. The ogre knows. Queen Olga knows, and somehow she destroyed the only way back to Never After.

'There's got to be another way,' says Gretel. 'There always is.'

'Right! Let's think,' says Filomena. 'How does one travel to a different world?'

'Wardrobes are usually good ways to get to places you need to go,' Jack offers.

'Or chimneys,' says Alistair.

'Or rabbit holes,' says Gretel. 'Wait, I think I remember Daddy telling us how he got here. He said he crossed some sort of bridge high up in the mountains above the city. As I recall, he said it's called the Bridge to Nowhere because people in the mortal world don't use it and don't know its true nature.'

'*The Bridge to Nowhere lies between the mountain plains. You'll get from there to here and here to there without taking a train*,' says Filomena, quoting from memory. 'I thought it was only in the books.'

'No, it's here in Los Angeles,' says Gretel. 'I'm pretty sure.'

'Let's see if we can find it online,' says Filomena, quickly tapping on her phone.

Sure enough, they discover that the Bridge to Nowhere is an abandoned bridge high up in the mountains east of the city.

'We'll need to take another cab, but I forgot to ask my parents for my allowance,' Filomena tells them.

'Not to worry,' says Gretel, flashing a hint of silver that's armour of a different kind. 'I have a credit card.'

Chapter Thirty-Two

Bridge Tolls and Trolls

The taxi lets them off at the foot of the mountain. There are no roads that lead to and from the Bridge to Nowhere – hence its name. Filomena's research states that the bridge was built between the canyons sometime in the 1930s, but a flood washed out the road, and it was never rebuilt. But Jack tells her that's not quite true. He says the bridge was always meant to be a portal, inaccessible except to those who knew where it truly led.

'But over in Never After it fell under the control of the ogres once they took Westphalia. We'll have to be careful when we get to the other side,' he cautions as they begin their steep hike up the winding path.

'So all we have to do is cross it and we're back?' asks Filomena, huffing from the weight of her backpack and the steep incline.

'Yep, and avoid being killed, of course,' says Jack.

'Easy peasy ogre squeezy,' Alistair scoffs. Ever since he beat the dragons' challenge, he's been a little cocky.

'Ogres!' Gretel shudders. 'Do we have to?'

'Unfortunately,' says Filomena.

Gretel laughs. Nothing seems to bring her down too much. As they make their way to the bridge, she asks them more about Never After. 'So have you guys met the fairies?'

'Only Zera,' says Filomena. 'She was cool, though.'

'Goblins?'

'I saw them around,' says Filomena. 'But I didn't get introduced.'

'One of my friends is a goblin. Great guy,' says Alistair. 'They get a bad rap.'

'Mermaids?' asks Gretel.

Alistair turns to Filomena. 'Wait, you guys don't have mermaids here, either?'

Filomena shakes her head, and then says, 'Nope. Gretel's right. No mermaids here.'

Now it's Alistair who looks sceptical. 'But I read something in the guidebook about a place here called SeaWorld. It said there are exhibits of all the largest and most impressive sea creatures. How could there not be a single mermaid?'

Filomena shrugs, and then says, 'We're taught to believe they don't exist.'

'Just like we're taught to believe that magic doesn't exist,' Gretel adds wistfully. 'It's sad how many believe it.'

Alistair huffs under the weight of Gretel's suitcase. 'Jeez, what do you have in this thing? A sleeping ogre?'

'Oh, no, that's just my make-up,' she says. 'And I packed light!'

'OK, I think we're getting close,' Filomena says as the path opens up to a view of the river below. The entrance to the bridge isn't much further.

'Oh, thank hooligans,' Alistair mumbles, still dragging the luggage with a strenuous effort even though it rolls. 'Hey, Gretel, is this your wheelhouse?' he asks, laughing at his own joke before she can even respond. 'Get it? Wheels . . .'

'Just ignore him,' Filomena suggests to Gretel.

As they make their way, Jack warns, 'Watch your step near the cliffside.' Some pebbles fall down the sheer drop.

'Thanks, Captain Obvious,' Filomena mumbles, passing by him at a brisk pace and leaving him dumbfounded at the nickname.

'Huh?' asks Jack.

She's nervous and crabby, and for some reason she finds Jack's cool demeanour irritating right now. Sure, he's a hero, but come on – all three of them passed the dragons' challenge. Filomena feels her annoyance rise, and she loses her footing on the cliff, only to have Jack catch her hand.

'Oh, thanks,' she says, now annoyed with herself instead of him.

Jack waits for Alistair to catch up. 'Did you hear that? Why would she call me Captain Something? She knows my name . . .'

Alistair is sweating under the hot sun and doesn't have the patience to try to make his friend feel better. 'I don't know. Girls are mean. And will you look at the size of this bag? What is make-up? What is she making up for?'

Filomena and Gretel arrive at the bridge first, but as they approach they see that it's blocked by a group of trolls. Trolls who are all too familiar to Filomena.

Except this time they are *literal* trolls. With hideous, deformed bodies and sharp teeth. They're still wearing the

Argyle Prep uniforms, the girls in tartan skirts and the boys in chinos and polo shirts.

'The Alfredos!' Filomena gasps. 'I knew it!'

'How odd that they're all named Alfredo,' says Gretel thoughtfully.

Filomena shakes her head, but she's too agitated to explain. Her suspicions were right! The Fettucine Alfredos *are* somehow tied to the books. And the Noodle Nuisances *aren't* just a group of snotty seventh-graders, apparently. They're literally a group of evil trolls.

She grabs Gretel from their line of sight, and the two of them hide behind the nearest tree. Filomena holds a finger to her lips and stares at Gretel, motioning for her to be quiet.

Filomena peers round the tree, glancing at the bridge again to see if it's really Posy and her nasty group of minions blocking the path to the portal. A brief look confirms her suspicions. Yup. It's definitely the Penne Posse. The girls are all there – Daisy, Petunia and Carnation – along with the boys, Tex, Angelo, Lake and Buck.

Her middle-school bullies are *actual trolls*. It's almost too good (or bad) to be true. She turns to Gretel and indicates her high heels. 'You might want to take those off,' Filomena whispers.

'Why?' Gretel whispers back.

Filomena responds by pointing to herself and to Gretel, and then using her index and middle fingers to portray a running motion.

No sooner does she finish conveying this information when they hear the sound of wheels being dragged along the rocky path. She needs to warn Jack and Alistair, but before she can, Alistair spots her, and his voice carries over the canyon.

Alistair yells, 'Hey, girls! Why are you hiding behind that tree?'

Filomena freezes against the tree, and Gretel quickly doffs her heels. But it's too late.

The jig, as they say, is up.

Posy turns her troll head 180 degrees and spots them immediately.

'THERE THEY ARE!' she yells in a deep roar.

There's no reason for hiding or pretending now.

'GET THEM!'

Once more, Filomena and her friends are running for their lives.

'So much cardio,' says Alistair in between huffs.

Filomena would laugh if she could, but she's too focused on getting away.

Chapter Thirty-Three

Kidnapped

They don't call him Jack the Giant Stalker because he's afraid of *trolls*. Next thing you know he'll be running from dwarves! The pint-sized monsters might seem frightening to his friends, but Jack finds them merely irritating. 'Get to the bridge!' he bellows. Then adds, 'The other way!' since they're running away from it.

Filomena stops first and looks back at him, hesitant.

The last time they were chased by this crew, she kept him from unleashing his magic on them. But there's no reason to stop him now; they're not just a bunch of seventh-graders. They're the ogres' minions.

'HURRY!' he yells again.

Filomena understands. 'To the bridge!' she orders, pulling on Gretel's sleeve and turning her round. 'Leave the bag!' she screams to Alistair.

'Nooooo!' Gretel protests. 'My make-up!'

'You don't need it! You're beautiful without it!' Filomena argues.

'You really are!' Alistair agrees, even as he tries to run with the large suitcase.

They run past Jack, who is standing at the edge of the cliff, his vines slipping out and reaching towards the trolls.

Alistair trips on a few rocks and falls down hard.

'OK, fine! Leave it!' Gretel finally agrees. They run towards the bridge and begin to cross to the other side. But Alistair, ever the gentleman, won't leave Gretel's bag behind and drags it behind him.

'JACK THE GIANT STALKER,' the troll formerly known as Posy Williamson sneers from the embankment. 'MORE LIKE JACK THE GIANT LOSER!'

The trolls fan out, wicked smiles on their faces. 'We knew you'd try to cross here once we cut down that stupid Heart Tree! You'll never get back to Never After now! You'll grow old and die here, just like your stupid mortal friend!'

'Is that you, Rumpelstiltskin?' Jack says. 'Haven't seen you since Queen Rosanna figured out your name! I thought that stench smelled familiar!'

Posy looks annoyed. 'I'm wearing deodorant!'

The vines from his arms uncoil ferociously and attack from above, and soon they've looped around each troll and rolled them up like . . . well, like spaghetti noodles.

But the trolls unleash their own weapons – garden shears! – and begin to hack at the vines.

Jack falls to his knees, his vines dripping blood.

'*Jack!*' Filomena cries, looking back and seeing him fall.

She and Gretel and Alistair have almost reached the end of the bridge, and even through the haze Filomena can see the familiar landscape of Never After ahead.

'GO!' yells Jack, keeping up the fight as new vines sprout to battle the trolls.

'No, we're not leaving without you!' cries Filomena. She removes the Dragon's Tooth sword from its sheath. 'Come on!' she tells the other two.

'Um, OK?' Gretel says, doing the same.

Alistair is already running towards the trolls, his dragon sword held high, Gretel's bag bumping behind him on the rocks. 'COME AND GET IT!' he screams.

Filomena lunges at the trolls, glad for the karate training

her parents made her take when she was in elementary school.

A few of the trolls focus their attention on the new combatants, and one of them slashes at Gretel's sweater.

'YOU ANIMALS! THIS IS DESIGNER!' Gretel yells as she stabs back and disappears into a troll pile.

Through the smoke and the blood and the yelling, Filomena loses track of her friends, but at last the trolls are choked unconscious by Jack's vines, and they fall, one by one.

Jack runs up to her, his vines coiled back round his arms. 'You all right?'

'Yeah. Where are Gretel and Alistair?'

'I thought they were with you!' says Jack.

'No!' says Filomena.

Then they see a group of trolls crossing the bridge, carrying two person-shaped bundles and one large suitcase above their heads.

Jack snaps his vines and sends them whizzing to catch the trolls, but they disappear into the haze at the end of the span just a moment before.

He curses roundly, using a few of those four-letter words Alistair taught him. 'Come on. We'll find them over there.'

They rush to the other side of the bridge, and as they pass through the portal, they find the bridge itself has changed and now they're running along a rickety wooden bridge staffed by ogres, just as Jack feared.

Jack pulls Filomena down, and they jump off, tumbling into a ditch underneath while an ogre army marches above them.

It's Jack's turn to shush her.

Filomena nods, her heart pounding. At last, when the ogres have disappeared round the bend, she and Jack come out of their hiding place and look around.

But there's no sign of the trolls — or of their friends.

They're gone.

Chapter Thirty-Four

Pub Meal

'They can't have got very far,' Filomena says, dusting herself off and getting up. She holds out a hand to help Jack to his feet.

He takes it gratefully. 'Hopefully not.'

'It's so strange,' says Filomena. 'All my life I thought my parents were exaggerating about child-snatchers and fairy abductions, but here we are and two of our friends have actually been snatched.'

'We'll get Alistair and Gretel back.'

'We have to,' says Filomena. 'Why did the trolls take them, anyway? Trolls don't eat . . . um . . . people, do they?'

'No, trolls are mostly vegetarian.'

'More like *carbo*-tarian,' says Filomena, remembering their penchant for buttered noodles. 'By the way, I keep meaning to tell you they're not all named Alfredo. It's a joke I made up for myself. I call them Fettucine Alfredos because that's all they eat. Noodles with butter and cream.'

'Pretty much the troll diet,' says Jack.

'Who knew?' she asks with a wan smile, which he returns. 'So do you think they were sent to the school to, uh, keep an eye on me or something?'

'Yeah,' says Jack. 'Someone knew you were there and who you really are.'

'But who am I?' asks Filomena. 'Even I don't know.'

'You're marked by Carabosse. You must be someone important,' says Jack, without looking her in the eye.

'Nah, I'm nobody,' says Filomena, wishing Jack wouldn't make such a sour face every time he says the evil fairy's name. Except Zera swore her sister wasn't evil, but Filomena didn't know *what* to believe.

'We're *all* nobody and somebody,' says Jack.

'OK, fine, but what do you think they want with Gretel and Alistair?'

'Mmm,' replies Jack with a shrug as he mulls the question.

'I guess her dad is rich,' says Filomena. 'He could pay a ransom, maybe?'

'Come on,' says Jack. 'Let's find out if anyone's seen them.'

They stop the first creature they encounter with a polite, 'Excuse me? Mr Gruff?'

The harried billy goat stops and turns to Jack. 'Yes?'

This is the biggest of the billy goats, Filomena realizes, almost as big as a horse. He's the famous billy goat who tossed the troll off the bridge.

'Have you seen a band of trolls leaving the bridge dragging two large bundles?'

'Trolls?' asks the billy goat. 'Hmm. I haven't seen a troll on the bridge since . . . well, you know.'

'They're small trolls. Dwarfish,' adds Filomena.

'Oh! Them I might have seen. They went that way,' the goat says, pointing his hoof in the direction of the woods.

Jack and Filomena shout their thanks and run to where the goat pointed. Jack kneels down in the dirt and inspects the tracks. 'They went this way, all right.'

But the tracks end near the river, and there are no tracks on the other side. Jack and Filomena question every creature they encounter, and look under every rock, inspect every ditch and scour every treetop, but there's no sign of their friends.

As darkness settles over the kingdom, Jack suggests they stop at a nearby village pub for a bite to eat and to rest for the night. There's no use looking for Alistair and Gretel in the dark. Unlike in her world, he explains, no decent business is conducted here once the sun has gone down, and they're sure to be robbed or attacked on the road. While Never After is imbued with magic, it doesn't have the one thing that makes the night safe in the mortal world: electricity.

Filomena is grateful. As worried as she is about their friends, her stomach is growling, and she'd like to lie down.

They make their way through the crowded, noisy establishment and find two seats at a long, empty table.

A ghoul with sockets for eyes and a half-transparent phantom-like appearance floats over, an apron round its midriff. 'Welcome to Dine, Drink and Die,' the spectre says lifelessly. 'What can we get for you this fine evening?'

'Two large bowls of Something Stew. And two mugs of Riotous Root Beer, good sir. And two rooms at the inn, if you've got them.'

'Excellent,' moans the ghoul, who disappears.

Filomena turns to Jack. 'Something Stew? Do you even know what's in it?'

'No one does. That's part of what makes it so appetizing.'

'OK,' she says, sounding sceptical. But then, anything's better than the vegan bologna sandwiches from the school cafeteria.

The ghoul eventually returns, first with their drinks and then with their bowls of stew.

'Now, that's a good spirit,' Jack says, flipping the ghoul a gold coin from his pocket.

The stew, as Jack promised, is delicious. While it isn't Zera's bountiful feast, there's something to be said for eating a mystery meal. Filomena tries to place the ingredients – bone broth for sure, and a variety of vegetables, spices and . . . tulips? She can't quite put a finger on it, but she eats everything.

'We've got to find them,' she says after wiping her mouth.

'We will, we will,' Jack reassures her. 'They can't have gone too far. It's dark now. They've had to stop and camp as well.'

'OK. But shouldn't we ask if anyone here has seen them?'

Jack sighs, then sets down his spoon and leaps on top the bench. 'Oi! Has anyone seen a bunch of trolls wandering around here? Dragging two person-shaped bundles?'

'And a suitcase!' Filomena adds.

Some pub patrons shake their heads and mutter to themselves, while others ignore Jack completely.

'Hmm . . . living or dead?' asks a serving ghoul.

'Living!' cries Filomena.

'Can't say we have,' the ghoul responds, wiping a table down. 'Sorry, lad.'

Jack shrugs, sits back down and finishes eating. 'They're not going to tell us anything – they're too scared of the ogres around here. And everyone knows the trolls work for the ogres.'

'Oh,' says Filomena as they head upstairs to turn in for the night. They have two rooms across the hall from each other.

She hopes Alistair and Gretel are OK. This is all her fault. The trolls were after her, and now her friends are paying for it. She's never felt so helpless and frustrated.

Inside her spare but clean room, she looks out of the window and up at a lone star in the sky, wishing her heart were as full as her belly.

Chapter Thirty-Five

Alistair Bartholomew Barnaby

Back on the road the next morning, Jack studies the tracks near the river more closely as a pixie flutters by. Filomena waves her down to ask if she's seen a group of trolls.

'Trolls?' the pixie repeats. 'I don't think I've seen trolls. I did see a lost girl, though.'

'Gretel!' yelps Filomena.

'Who is she?' asks the pixie.

'She's the Cobbler's daughter,' Jack explains.

The fairy gasps. 'As in . . . *the* Cobbler? He's back?'

'Not quite,' says Jack.

'Could you please tell us where you last saw her?' Filomena begs. 'It's really important.'

'Hmm,' the pixie coos, pointing in every direction as she flits above them. 'I saw her opposite of west; she was not dressed the best. Perhaps on foot, bare and bloody. Distressed and dirty, though fair even while muddy. Lost but soon to be found, sitting on the ground.'

With that, she takes off into the sky, soaring with poise and ease. She pauses and yells back to them, 'Please tell the Cobbler to make me a pretty new pair of flats if you see him! Pointy and green, to match my wings!'

Then she shrinks until she vanishes from their sight.

'I hope Gretel's OK. Do you think the trolls let her go?' Filomena asks. 'It seems so unlikely.'

'I was wondering the same thing,' Jack replies. 'Anyway, the pixie said she saw her opposite of west, which is this way. Let's go.'

He turns east and Filomena follows close behind, both all but running as they shout Gretel's name into the air, listening for an answer in the breeze.

'Here! I'm over here!' comes Gretel's unmistakeable voice.

'Gretel!' Filomena exclaims once she sees her friend, who is sprawled on the ground and looks a bit worse for wear. Gretel stands and Filomena hugs her tightly. 'Are you OK?'

Gretel is dishevelled and exhausted but mostly seems annoyed by the whole experience. 'I'm totally fine. Stupid trolls.'

'What happened?'

'Well, they carried us here. I heard splashing, so I figured we went through some sort of river. When we got to this bank, they let me go. They just dropped me. A couple of them were whining about having to carry me and my bag. Said I was useless and heavy, and so the leader said to just leave me.' She shrugs. 'Stupid trolls. They all need makeovers.'

'What about Alistair?' asks Jack. 'Where is he?'

'They kept Alistair. They think he has something they want – I heard them. They kept saying something about the treasure, the treasure . . . the wishes that promise pleasure . . .'

'Treasure . . . and wishes?' asks Filomena. 'Why would Alistair have those?'

Jack shuffles his feet and looks down at the ground.

Filomena raises her eyebrows. 'The trolls were talking about Aladdin's lamp, weren't they? You said the ogres were looking for it, that they invaded Parsa in search of it.'

She shrugs off her backpack and takes out the Never After book with the lamp on the front cover. She stares at the pages. 'The books always hint that Alistair is not quite who he appears to be. I figured we'd find out in the thirteenth book. And this *is* the thirteenth book. We're in it.'

'What's she talking about?' asks Gretel.

Jack doesn't answer. Finally he mouths, *Long story.*

'This isn't the first time the ogres tried to take Alistair, either,' says Filomena, feeling a rush of certainty. 'It's not a coincidence. They know who he is. *You* know who he is.' She glares at Jack.

Jack looks miserably guilty. 'We didn't mean to deceive you.'

'In the books, after Aladdin's wedding, the lamp is placed back in the good care and keeping of Ali Baba,' says Filomena.

'Come again?' asks Gretel.

'Alistair Bartholomew Barnaby,' says Filomena. 'Alistair is Ali Baba! He has the lamp!'

'Well, not quite,' says Jack. 'But he is the key to finding it. All they have to do is point him to the right cave and he can say the magic words.'

'Cave! That's where they're taking him. Some kind of cave they found in the deserts of . . . Parsa?' says Gretel.

'But why do the ogres want the lamp? Why do they

need so badly to make a wish?'

'Who knows? All we *do* know is that we have to get to Alistair and the lamp before they do,' says Jack. 'And remember what the dragons said? We'll need the wolves to defeat the ogres. Maybe we should ask them to help us now.'

For once, Filomena doesn't argue.

Prologue

The Unknown

The tales told of this day say Carabosse cursed the kingdom. The tales told of this day say Carabosse disappeared, never to be seen again. But the tales don't tell us everything.

As the blood dripped from her hand, Carabosse finished the blessing within her curse.

'This I promise all of you
When twisted tales are finally told true –
The ogres' rule will end –
And those left standing will be my friends.'

The court exploded in chaos and confusion. The fairies

disappeared first, and the dragons followed. But the rest were not so fast or so lucky. They fell into slumber as the curse worked its magic.

The tales told of this day don't say that Queen Olga rose from her chair, a hideous beast, that she leaped for Carabosse, hungry for her niece. That Queen Olga had a response to the curse, a reply also steeped in verse.

'A thousand nights and a thousand days I have waited –

So this moment shall not be abated –

I have waited far too long,

I shall not be stymied by your song.

A royal babe, a fairy halfling, this was a feast for the taking.

With her blood there's no mistaking –

My power invincible, my reach unstoppable –

And all will know and bow and worship

Olga of Orgdale. Forever and ever

And Never After.

Carabosse, you shall be forgotten,

Reviled and loathsome,

And all shall call you EVIL.'

The ogre queen bared her fangs and her claws and

leaped to snatch the babe from Carabosse's arms. But the fairy was faster.

'You are right, witch of Orgdale.

None shall know what truly happened today.

My name, my reputation, you are welcome to slay.

But you shall not have my sister's babe.

By my love, you shall never find her.

My magic will hide her.

Unless there is a force stronger than you.

Until then I bid you adieu.'

And with those words, the fairy Carabosse was never seen again.

Part Four

Wherein . . .

Filomena dons a red cloak to call the Wolves of the Wood.

The friends journey to the Kingdom of the Lamp.

They once again face an Ogre's Wrath.

Chapter Thirty-Six

Into the Woods

'I'm sorry I didn't tell you before,' says Jack, 'but it's been difficult to figure out whom to trust. When Zera found out that the ogres were looking for the lamp, that's when she sent Alistair to me. I'm supposed to keep him safe from them. Obviously, I failed.'

'They don't have the lamp yet,' Filomena says. 'It's not too late.'

'Lamp schwamp,' says Gretel. 'If we're going to rally these wolves on our side, we should get going.' She inspects Filomena's outfit and begins to fidget with the fit of the hoodie Filomena is wearing over the dragonskin armour.

She pulls the waist drawstrings together tightly. 'There.'

'Ugh, I like it loose.'

'But it looks better this way,' argues Gretel.

'No means no,' says Filomena, untying the strings and wearing it slouchy and baggy once more.

'Hopeless,' says Gretel with a sigh.

'Right,' says Jack, ignoring their bickering and leading the way. 'We'll have to go deeper into the Great Forest to find the wolves.'

'But aren't wolves evil?' asks Filomena as they disappear into the shade of the forest. 'Why would we even *want* their help? Won't they try to eat us or something?'

Jack looks at Filomena with confusion on his face. 'Eat us? They're not ogres.'

'Evil? Wolves? Why would you think that?' asks Gretel. 'I grew up on the mortal side, and even I know wolves aren't evil.'

'They're not?' asks Filomena.

'Wolves are the most noble creatures in Never After,' says Jack.

'But what about the Big Bad Wolf?' asks Filomena. 'The one who's always blowing down the three pigs' houses?'

'Is that what you think? The tales truly are twisted. The

wolf has let those pigs live on his land forever. They're his tenants.'

'But I heard them talk about the wolf. "Now, if he arrives, you need to get to my house immediately," the pig wearing a suit said.'

'Because that pig always hosts. You didn't hear the rest of the sentence, which was "where I'll be serving the hors d'oeuvres",' says Jack. 'And his food is so good, it always blows them away.'

Filomena shakes her head. 'But what about Little Red Riding Hood?'

'What about her?' asks Gretel, intrigued.

'The Big Bad Wolf dressed up as her grandmother and ate both of them, but the hunter saved them,' she says, telling them the story as she's always known it.

Jack and Gretel stare at Filomena in silent disbelief for a moment, exchanging stumped glances with each other. Finally Jack can't take it any longer.

'The hunter saved them?' he repeats as if he can't believe what he heard.

'Didn't he?'

'No . . .' Even Gretel is shaking her head.

'That's not the true story. At all,' says Jack firmly.

'Yeah,' Gretel chimes in. 'Even I know that isn't the

true story. My father's told me enough times. He said the mortals get all the fairy tales wrong. It drives him crazy.'

'Whoever is telling these tales is telling them wrong for a reason,' says Jack. 'Didn't you say that's why you read the Never After books? To read the "real story"?'

Filomena considers it. The Never After books must not have reached that part of the story yet. 'I guess you're right. But if the wolf isn't bad, then what about the hunter? Isn't the hunter the hero of the story?'

'Oh goodness, no,' says Gretel as both she and Jack shudder at the mention of the hunter.

'Why?' ask Filomena. 'What's wrong with the hunter?'

'Here, *hunter* is another word for *ogre*,' Jack explains. 'Because ogres eat and hunt us.'

'Trust us on this one,' says Gretel.

Jack turns to Gretel. 'If we're going to call the wolves, she's going to need a red cloak,' he says.

'On it,' says Gretel. 'Hand me my bag.' She searches through her suitcase and pulls out a bit of plain red fabric. Other colours of the rainbow slide out with it, and she pushes them back inside for safekeeping. 'I always keep extra fabric with me, just in case.'

'You have a sewing kit and fabric in your bag? No

wonder it's so heavy!' says Filomena. 'I thought you just had make-up.'

Gretel shrugs. 'And a few other things.'

They rest in the shade so Gretel can sew. 'You know, this sort of thing usually takes a lot of time and effort,' she tells them as she grabs her scissors and cuts the material in two. One piece is smaller than the other. 'But I'll do my best.' Then she starts to sew, stitching the blood-red cloth with a needle and thread.

After just a few minutes of quick work, Gretel holds up a little hooded red shawl, shaking it in front of Filomena. 'Take off your hoodie and put this on. Trust me. I know it's not the most glamorous, or even a full cloak, but we have to make do with what I've got.'

Filomena does as she's told, exchanging her favourite and most comfortable hoodie for the red cloak.

Gretel rummages in her suitcase and comes up with a little basket for Filomena to hold. 'Little Red Riding Hood,' she declares with satisfaction. 'Off to see the wolf in the woods.'

Chapter Thirty-Seven

To Grandma's House

Filomena walks deeper into the forest with slow, timid footsteps. She steps on a twig and startles, almost dropping her basket. Jack and Gretel are following behind, but she can't see or hear them, so she might as well be all alone in this dark and scary place.

Her only comfort is that she's *somewhat* prepared – wearing the dragonhide armour and the Dragon's Tooth sword in her sheath. At least she can defend herself against anything she might come across. Jack told her not to hesitate and to stab hard if she's attacked.

The forest is darker with every step, the trees casting

eerie shadows, and the rustling of woodland creatures is ominous rather than soothing. Filomena feels many unseen eyes watching her. But Jack told her this is the only way to catch the wolves' attention; they hardly ever leave the forest.

She pushes down her fear and swings the basket over her arm cheerfully, putting on a brave face and forcing a smile. Then she calls out innocently, 'Here I am alone, walking to Grandma's house.'

Gretel says it's the code to call out the wolves and ask them for help. But in the fairy tale version Filomena knows, the wolves *ate* the little girl and her grandmother. Yet here she is, out in a dark, scary forest alone at night, in search of the wolves.

If my parents could see me now, she thinks.

She waits a few beats for any sign of movement, any rustle among the bushes. But nothing happens. No sounds come, no howling of any sort. No gigantic paws running straight for her. No response at all.

She frowns and starts traipsing through the woods, almost in a skip. 'I hope Grandma is expecting me!' she yells, trying to sound as sweet and naive as possible.

When there is no reply, Filomena starts to question her acting skills. She also begins to wonder if the wolves are even out here. *Shouldn't they have found me by now? How slow* are *these things?*

She stops walking forward and turns round. Enough is enough. She's done with the whole charade. She walks back in the direction from which she came, peering around in the darkness for a glimpse of Jack or Gretel. But it's so dark she can hardly see a thing aside from what's directly in front of her.

Mumbling to herself, she stumbles over a rock and swipes her knee against a tree trunk. When she bends to brush off her knee, the basket tumbles, spilling items on to the ground. With an irritated huff, she squats and starts picking them up. Gretel will be annoyed if she's lost any of her sewing supplies. Finding tiny needles and buttons and bobbins in the dark is harder than it seems, and Filomena feels around for anything she may have missed. Once she's gathered everything, she stands up and looks around.

OK, guys, you can come out now. This is getting old. You could have helped me pick up all that stuff . . .

She crosses her arms and taps her foot, waiting for her friends to emerge from somewhere, anywhere, in the black.

Just as she's about to yell that they should quit playing

around, a deep and blood-curdling voice cuts into the silence.

'Are you lost, little girl?' someone asks just behind her.

The hair on the back of her neck stands to attention. Then, after a shudder, she realizes she's being silly and quickly recovers. *There's nothing to be scared of. The wolves are the most noble creatures of Never After. Jack said so. The wolves are good.*

Plus, she's grateful not to be alone any more. At last they've found what they're looking for. She turns to smile, but the smile dies on her lips the moment she turns around.

Because standing there, towering above her with huge fangs and hungry eyes, is not a wolf.

It's a hunter.

Chapter Thirty-Eight

Hunter and Hunted

It's a monstrous ogre, drool dripping from his front teeth. You'd think Filomena would be used to seeing ogres by now, considering she turned one of them into mush a few chapters back. But ogres tend to take the breath out of you.

Finally she finds her voice. 'I was just on my way to Grandma's house!' she says, taking a few steps back from the disgusting creature and hoping the wolves will show themselves as soon as possible. 'My grandma is waiting for me!'

The ogre laughs a heartless laugh. 'I'll eat your granny too!'

The terror starts at her toes, travels up her legs, through her gut and straight to her heart. She has nowhere to run, nowhere to hide. And her friends are nowhere to be found. Where in fairyland are those wolves, anyway? They might as well be fictional, for all the help she's received from them.

Noble creatures, my nose.

If only she could think of a spell, but all she can focus on is staying alive and uneaten. And hoping that wherever Jack and Gretel are, this hunter didn't get to them first.

I would have heard them scream, right?

Right.

The ogre sniffs the air. 'You smell like you taste good.'

'No,' Filomena blurts out, adamantly shaking her head. 'I taste horrible. Trust me.' She points a finger in the other direction and adds, 'An ogre down the road sampled me earlier and spat out the bit he tried.'

He narrows his eyes, like he's considering her statement. Then he grunts with finality, having decided. 'Liar.'

'No! I swear!' she insists. 'There was a much more delicious person wandering in the woods over that way!' She points again, and the ogre turns in that direction.

Please be dumb enough to believe me. Please be—

But the ogre has turned back to her, and this time, he's

rooting around in his pockets. He finally removes what looks like . . . *a fork!*

Filomena screams and tries to run, but her feet are frozen to the ground.

The ogre puts a heavy hand on her shoulder, holding her still, and says, 'I use this one on little rodents and liars like you.'

'Filomena!' Jack's voice rings out as he emerges in the darkness, with Gretel at his heels.

'No! Run away! Save yourselves!' Filomena demands of her friends.

But the ogre moves first, reaching to stab the fork into Filomena's stomach.

She closes her eyes, waiting to feel the life drain out of her. But there is only a small click, a tap from a blunt, three-pronged jab.

The dragonhide armour! The fork couldn't penetrate it! Not one bit.

The stupefied hunter lets out a 'Huh?' when she doesn't drop to the ground dead, as he intended.

While he tries to figure out how she managed to withstand a fork wound, Filomena reaches into her pocket for the fang she received from the dragons.

'Hey! I use this one on big, foolish traitors like you.'

Without any more thought or hesitation, Filomena stabs the ogre with the Dragon's Tooth, hard and fast in his thigh.

He stumbles back in surprise on his clumsy and oversized feet. As he does, a pack of wolves emerges from the shadows, galloping closer with gallant ferocity. The wolves attack, biting and nipping at the ogre's haunches, and Filomena takes the opportunity to roll away to safety.

One ogre is no match for the snarling wolves, and at last the monster runs away and the wolves give chase until he's out of their forest.

When the wolves return, they turn their attention to Filomena. The Wolves of the Wood circle her, howling in unison.

Her heartbeat picks up again as she wonders whether she's just escaped from an ogre only to be torn apart by these savage beasts. The wolves continue to circle and howl.

'Please! I've come to seek your aid!' says Filomena.

The wolves stop circling, and one by one they bow to her, stretching down, showing the scruffs of their necks, and all at once they transform into a group of raggedy-looking kids.

The tallest one, their leader – a handsome, dark-haired

lad who looks to be about thirteen – nods to her just as Gretel and Jack arrive at last.

'You're all right!' says Gretel, enveloping Filomena in a hug. 'That armour's something else, huh?'

'Stabbed him hard!' says Jack. 'Just like I told you – good girl!'

Filomena is so relieved, it's too hard to laugh. But it's difficult to ignore the wolf pack of boys and girls.

'You called for aid,' says their leader 'We answered. We are the Wolves of the Wood. I'm Rolf. This is Rox. That's Sid, Eddie, Gina and Max.' Introductions are made all around.

'You're Jill's brother, right?' asks Rolf, shaking Jack's hand.

'Cousin,' Jack corrects with a smile. 'Our mothers were sisters. How'd you know Jill?'

Rolf nods. 'She rolled our way a while back. Said she was headed to the beach, wanted to be near the water. And who might you be?' he asks Gretel.

'Gretel,' says Gretel. 'Nice to meet you.'

Jack leans in and whispers, 'She's the Cobbler's daughter.'

'*The* Cobbler?' Rolf asks, head still slightly turned to Jack.

Gretel looks pleased. 'Yup.'

'Your dad makes the best leather jackets,' says Rolf.

'I'll be sure to tell him that,' says Gretel. 'He's retired now. He lives in Boca mostly.'

'Grandma is always talking about moving to Boca!' says Rox.

'Ahem,' says Filomena. 'I hate to interrupt, but we've got something important to ask you guys.'

'Spill it, Red,' says Rolf. The other wolves gather around to listen.

'We need your help to find our friend. A bunch of evil trolls snatched him, and they're holding him hostage somewhere,' she tells them.

'Trolls, huh?' says Rolf. 'I think some of them just passed this way. Nasty little critters.'

'Definitely smelled them earlier,' agrees Sid, scrunching his nose.

'That would be them,' says Jack with a grim smile.

Rolf appears to think over their request.

'Dude, if we're going to do this, we should bounce,' says Max. 'We chased that ogre away, but no doubt he'll be back soon. And most likely with a bunch of his ugly friends. We should get out of here pronto.'

'So, um, you'll help us?' Filomena asks. 'Please?'

The wolves look at each other, and Rolf finally responds on behalf of the entire pack. 'Of course we will. We always answer to the one who wears the Red Cloak.'

Chapter Thirty-Nine

The Kingdom of the Lamp

Rolf and the other wolves discuss strategies for finding the trolls. 'Our scouts say the trolls you're looking for went east after leaving the forest.'

'East? That means they definitely headed to Parsa,' says Jack.

'Is that bad?' asks Filomena, sensing something in Jack's tone.

'It's just . . . there's no reason to go to Parsa unless . . .'

'Unless?' she prods.

'Unless they've discovered the hidden cavern where the lamp is hidden,' says Jack.

'That would not be good,' says Filomena.

'No,' Jack agrees.

'Maybe Alistair can stall them,' says Gretel.

'Let's hope,' says Filomena. 'How far away is Parsa from here?'

Rolf calculates in his head. 'At least a day.'

'On foot?' asks Gretel, looking worriedly at her shoes.

'Oh, no,' says Rox, soothing Gretel. 'Wolves ride.'

Rolf grins. He puts two fingers in his mouth and whistles sharply.

On cue, a group of wolves join them in the clearing, this time driving motorcycles. They hand out helmets, goggles and leather jackets.

'You know how to drive one of these things?' Rolf asks Jack while shrugging on his jacket. It has *BIG BAD WOLF* embroidered on the back.

'Er . . .' says Jack. 'We mostly have donkeys in Vineland.'

'I know how!' says Filomena. 'Dad takes me off-roading all the time.'

Filomena puts on a helmet and goggles that are a little too big for her face. 'Hang on,' she tells Jack, who gingerly steps behind her on to the nearest bike.

Gretel gets a ride with Gina, who asks, 'You good back there?'

Gretel is making sure the helmet doesn't mess up her hair too much. She gives Gina a thumbs-up. 'Go fast!' she urges.

The wolves, with their three new riders, zoom out of the forest and into the desert.

They reach the fringes of Parsa and stop at an outlying village to ask if anyone has seen a band of trolls and one hostage. Filomena marvels at the market in the square, which, Jack explains, is a thousand-year old souk. As soon as they get off their motorbikes, they are accosted by merchants cheerfully and aggressively hawking rugs, candy, kaftans.

'I'll give you good price,' offers one, holding up a patterned rug.

'Have you seen a group of trolls with a kid?' asks Jack. 'About this high, and sort of a loudmouth?'

The merchant gives him a sly look. 'It'll cost you.'

Jack grumbles but pays up.

'Over there, by the lamps,' the seller says, hooking a thumb to the other side of the market.

But there are a dozen stalls selling lamps of all kinds, which glitter and shine in the dimness of each tent. Lamps shaped like globes, lamps as tall as trees, lamps hanging from trees. They hear Alistair before they see him.

They creep to the tent where he's being held and peek in.

'I told you, I don't know where it is!' he says crossly to the group of trolls in school uniforms. 'I have no idea.'

Jack, Filomena and Gretel exchange excited glances, relief evident on their faces. Rolf points to Alistair questioningly. The three of them nod. *That's him.*

'Honestly, he's as useless as the other one,' one of the trolls grumbles.

Gretel huffs. Filomena pinches her to be quiet.

'Get rid of him,' says another troll.

'No! He's supposed to know where it is! Maybe we can pull out his eyes, and then he'll talk.'

'He's no use to us blind!'

Gretel squeals in fear.

'Shhh,' says Filomena. Before she can turn to Rolf and the wolves to ask them about the rescue plan, Alistair falls backwards from his chair and disappears from sight.

The trolls look around, agitated.

'Where'd he go?'

'Barnacles!'

'Now what!'

But the wolves, suddenly holding an Alistair-sized bag,

signal their new friends while running to their bikes. They all zoom off away from the village and back to the desert. When they're a safe distance, Rolf gives the signal to stop.

The wolf who carried the sack on his bike dumps out Alistair upside down. 'Ow! Watch it!'

'This *is* the boy you were looking for, right?' Rolf asks, raising a thick dark eyebrow.

Filomena laughs, understanding the implication behind the question. 'Yes!'

'Loud little horror,' says the wolf who brought him in. 'Kept screaming all the way here.'

'Be nice, Sid.'

Alistair stands up, dusting off his trousers. 'Was that truly necessary, sir?' he asks Sid. Then he sees Rolf. 'Oh! You're the Big Bad!' he says. 'Cor blimey, I thought you lot never left the forest!'

'Only to answer the call,' says Rolf with a smile. 'Otherwise we stay in the forest. Someone's got to keep the ogres out, after all, and take care of Grandma.'

'Alistair! You're all right!' says Filomena, giving him a fierce hug.

'No worse for the wear,' says Alistair with a smile. 'Hi, Gretel. Jack.'

'Hey, bud,' Jack says.

'You're still wearing your armour,' says Gretel.

'Yes, very useful. The trolls couldn't do anything to me.' He turns to Jack. 'Don't worry. I didn't tell them where it is.'

'Good. But since we're here, we should secure it and bring it back to Zera,' says Jack. 'That's what we were trying to do when we were here last, but then the ogres came and we had to run.'

'They chased us off that cliff over there,' Alistair tells the others. 'Good thing Jack had the Pied Pipe.'

'I knew there was a Heart Tree in the ravine, so we just had to jump to it,' says Jack.

'And you ended up in my world,' says Filomena.

'Oh? What world would that be? Where are you from, Red?' asks Rolf.

'The mortal one,' says Gretel. 'I'm from there too. Although I was born here.'

Rox asks her, 'What's it like?'

'Shiny,' says Gretel. 'It's like here, but with freeways instead of forests.'

'Open road,' says Rolf. 'I like the sound of that.'

'Maybe when all this is over, you guys can come see for yourself,' says Gretel.

The wolves say they like the sound of that.

Filomena clears her throat again. She needs them to focus. 'OK, now we have Alistair back, so thank you. But that's not all we need to do.'

'We've got to finish what we started,' adds Jack. 'We have to get the lamp, to make sure Queen Olga doesn't get her hands on it.'

'Oh, is that all?' quips Sid.

'And you guys know where this lamp is?' asks Rox.

'Wasn't it hidden away after Aladdin's wedding?' says Gina.

Alistair nods. 'It was. My family hid it. I'm the only person who knows where it is.'

The wolves look impressed.

'All right, we're in,' says Rolf. 'Those ogres are a nuisance. We'll do anything to get rid of them once and for all. Lead the way.'

'Righto,' says Alistair. He purses his lips and whistles a peculiar melody. At first, nothing happens. Then from afar comes the sound of the wind rushing towards them, faster and faster. When Filomena turns her head, she has to duck whatever is making that sound as it flies past her.

When it stops, it hovers in the air beside Alistair.

Wait a minute. Is that a—?

'Ah, here we go!' Alistair says, pleased with himself. 'Yes, it's my magic carpet. Much faster than those motorbikes, eh?'

Sid rolls his eyes. Rolf looks impressed. Jack grins at his friend. Filomena stares in disbelief at the Arabian rug floating in the sky.

'Well, don't be shy,' Alistair says, petting the carpet like a good boy. 'Everyone on.'

'Can we all fit?' asks Gretel.

'Hmm,' Alistair replies. 'It only seats two comfortably, three if you must. Hang on a tick.' He points to the wolves, counting them, plus his three friends. Then he mutters a spell under his breath, and the rug multiplies into four carpets, all the same length and width as the original. 'All right, that should do it.'

Jack doesn't hesitate to walk forward, but he pauses before he climbs on to the carpet that has lowered itself near his feet. He turns to Filomena and holds out his hand.

He really does have the nicest manners.

She steps forward and takes his hand, letting him help her on to the carpet. He joins her, followed by Alistair. She cosies herself into a cross-legged position and touches the soft fabric.

Once the entire group is situated, Alistair pats the carpet again and says, 'To the Kingdom of the Lamp, please.' And then over his shoulder he tosses, 'Hold tight, everyone!'

The carpets take off with impressive speed and precision, and they glide through the sky effortlessly. Filomena clings to the frayed ends of the rug, her hair flapping in the wind.

After a time, they start to drift down, lower and lower, until they can see the skyline of a large city.

Alistair stretches his arms wide, motioning to the scene below. 'We're here. Welcome to the Kingdom of the Lamp.'

Filomena takes in the gorgeous landscape with awe. The city before her is sprawling and pink, with turrets and minarets and low-slung buildings around a centre square where a large and boisterous souk is set up. 'I thought Parsa was destroyed.'

'Invaded and under ogre rule, but not destroyed, no,' says Jack. 'Alistair, we should set down somewhere inconspicuous, huh?'

'Oh, right,' says Alistair, and he directs the rugs to fly low towards a nearby alley.

The carpets land them safely and gently in an empty

side alley, just past the busy marketplace, which buzzes with voices and laughter.

'All right, where's the lamp?' Filomena asks.

'Lamp?' says Alistair. 'Oh, the lamp's not here. Out in the far desert. Miles and miles away. But I thought we'd get something to eat first. I'm starving. The only thing the trolls fed me was soggy noodles.'

Chapter Forty

Desert Trek

'We've stopped for a snack?' Jack is beside himself.
'Well, technically it's lunchtime. So we'll
need more than a snack,' says Alistair, unperturbed.

'What part of this-is-an-urgent-mission don't you
understand?' snaps Jack. 'Those wolves are right. That
ogre is going to come back and bring his friends with him.
They're probably following us right now.'

'Relax – you're paranoid,' says Alistair. 'Ever since you
killed that giant, you see ogres everywhere.'

'They *are* everywhere,' Jack argues. 'If you haven't
noticed, they've practically taken over all of Never After.'

But Alistair won't be dissuaded. 'Ogres can't run that fast. What part of I-haven't-eaten-in-two-days don't you understand?' he asks as he heads to the nearest food stall. He turns back to them with his hands on his hips. 'You all probably stopped at an inn, didn't you?'

'Well . . .' says Filomena, hedging on how much to admit.

'And had Something Stew and Riotous Root Beers?' accused Alistair. 'I smelled it as the trolls carried me past the river.'

'It was dark!' says Jack. 'We had to stop somewhere.'

'Just like we're stopping now,' says Alistair.

'What's going on?' asks Rolf. 'Where's the cave?'

'Alistair is . . . having lunch,' says Jack through gritted teeth.

'Oh! Lunch! And shopping!' Gretel claps her hands as she looks around the souk.

'Gretel hasn't eaten, either,' says Filomena, surrendering. 'We probably should stop to have a bite.' After all, the sizzling smells of the market are tempting and hard to ignore.

The wolves fan out into the souk, following their bellies. Rolf shrugs. 'Sorry. We don't get much in the forest. Even Grandma's food gets tired after a while. But if the ogres did follow us here, we'll be sure to sniff them out.'

Jack knows he's outnumbered. 'Fine. Fine. We're stopping for lunch. Fine.'

Rolf catches up with his pack.

Gretel loops her arm through Filomena's. 'Let's go get lunch and then look around. I look a wreck after my kidnapping.'

'This way!' says Alistair.

Jack shakes his head and follows his friends into the market. Just as at the village souk, merchants of all kinds try to tempt shoppers with their wares, and even the food stalls are filled with salesmen seeking to lure diners. Before they can object, the four of them are seated at benches around a nearby table, plates piled high with bread and cheese in front of them.

'Oooh, they have lamb kebabs,' says Alistair, who's practically drooling as he reads the menu. He orders for the table, and soon there's a proper feast of chicken, lamb, and steak kebabs, along with saffron-scented biryani, onion and tomato salads, and five kinds of hummus.

After lunch, Gretel and Filomena wander through the stalls. Gretel looks for just the perfect kaftan – 'I need something light and breathable, but also exquisite,' she decides.

Jack reminds them to hurry and to watch out for ogres. Alistair goes his own way, muttering something about camels.

The girls meander through the busy street market, stopping to glance at women's clothing hung loosely on racks outside various shops and tents. They're stopped several times by vendors trying to sell them overpriced goods, and Gretel firmly shakes her head once, eyeing what they're offering.

Finally, they stop at a small tent whose opening is hung with beads. They rattle and chime as Gretel goes in, but Filomena stops. She notices that Alistair has gone to see a man about a camel. The gentleman offers camel-back rides through the desert, and Alistair has taken him aside and they are speaking quietly.

'Filomena! Come see this! I think I found the one!' Gretel exclaims from inside.

'Coming,' Filomena calls, taking her eyes from Alistair and walking through the beaded entrance of the tent.

Gretel holds up a cream-and-aqua kaftan with an intricate bead pattern on the front, wiggling it for Filomena to examine. 'What do you think?'

'It's really pretty,' Filomena says, and she means it. The

dress looks like it belongs on a princess, and for Gretel it's perfect.

Filomena waits while Gretel barters with the vendor, trading some of her sewing items and fabric for the dress. Once the exchange is made, Gretel skips to the back section of the tent to change. There's a folding wall, giving customers an area where they can try the garments on in privacy.

Gretel keeps her armour on underneath, but now instead of a torn and dirty jumpsuit, she's wearing a floaty kaftan. 'How do I look?' she asks with a twirl.

'You look great,' Filomena states, linking their arms once again and heading out of the tent. 'I'm sure you'll find a handsome prince who'll love it. And you.'

Gretel laughs. 'I was just kidding about looking for a prince earlier. I don't need a prince. I've taken over my dad's business, and it's doing so much better than it ever has. I'm my own princess already.'

'You really are,' says Filomena, feeling a rush of warmth for her friend.

They join Alistair and Jack, who are waiting with the wolves by the camels. Alistair informs the group that the camels will take them where they need to go.

'Camels?' asks Rolf.

303

'Yes, it's the only way through the dunes. The bikes will sink in the sand.'

There's a little grumbling from the wolves, but soon they're on their camels. Alistair leads the way, the other camels trailing his as they take off towards the vast desert.

'Am I the only one who realizes that wolves are riding on camels?' Sid whines. 'They are completely unnecessary.'

'Actually,' Alistair cuts in curtly, 'they are necessary. These are the Baba family camels, the only ones who know the way to the secret cave. You can't get there without them.' The sun beats down on them. Filomena loses track of time, unable to guess how long they've been riding across the hot, empty desert.

Gretel starts to complain of thirst. 'Why would we *ever* go into a desert without at least one bottle of water?' she whines.

'We'll be fine,' Alistair says confidently. 'The cavern isn't too far from here, I think.' Then he whispers, 'I hope.'

Moments later, as though he somehow jinxed them, gusts of wind kick up around the riders, whipping their hair back. The squalls send sand flying every which way, into their eyes and against their bodies, pelting them with painful prickles. They try to shield their eyes with their arms as the winds snake and bend, ravaging the previously calm and monotonous landscape. The sudden windstorm makes the dry heat and intense sun feel even worse, increasing the overall discomfort tenfold.

'What's happening?' Filomena yells.

'Just follow me! It's a desert defence mechanism! Which means we're getting close to the secret cavern!' Alistair shouts back. 'Everyone, try to stay calm and don't panic! We just need to get past the oasis, and then we're there!'

They fight their way through the sandstorm, the camels steadfastly moving forward. At last the winds die down, and they find themselves in the middle of a green oasis. Palm trees surround a sparkling pond and comfortable tents with tables full of fruit and water.

'We can stop for a drink of water, but we can't stay long,' says Alistair.

'Why not?' asks Gretel.

'Because then we'll never be able to leave,' he explains. 'The oasis is enchanted to keep people here and dissuade looters from trying to find the cave.'

The members of the group quickly help themselves to refreshments. Filomena is sceptical of the enchantment at first but then feels the spell working on her. How nice it would be to sit in that lounge chair by the water. Why, she would never want to leave! Then she realizes she has to snap out of it.

'Let's go, let's go!' says Alistair as Jack tries to help hustle the others out of the tents and back on to the camels.

The wolves grumble, and Rolf strives to keep them together. 'Come on, come on, no time to rest, let's go.'

When they're beyond the spell of the oasis, Filomena feels sharper and in her right mind once more.

The camels keep their steady pace, and for hours the riders journey in the blazing heat until they come to a rocky mountain rising up from the sands and blocking their way.

Alistair stops right in front of it, and the rest of the group does the same.

'Is this it?' calls Jack.

'Are we here?' asks Filomena, shielding her eyes.

'You'd better hurry up,' says Rolf, who's sniffing the air suspiciously. 'I smell ogre.'

The wolves tense and everyone looks around, but the desert is, well, deserted. There's no one for miles, at least that they can see.

Filomena cranes her neck in every direction, but she sees only the blindingly bright sand dunes. She hopes that if ogres followed them out here, maybe they've sunk into the sand.

'I didn't just stop here for no reason,' Alistair huffs, getting off his camel and walking to the mountain's rocky wall. 'Open sesame!' he commands.

There is a squeak and then a dull roar as the door to the cavern opens slowly.

Chapter Forty-One

The Cavern

Alistair looks pleased. 'We'll leave the camels here and go the rest of the way on foot.'

'Me and Rox are going to stay out here,' says Sid, looking suspiciously at the dark cavern. 'Stand guard.'

'Good plan,' says Rolf approvingly. 'The rest of you, come with me.'

Jack removes the Seeing Eye from his pocket. Its light casts a dim glow into the dark cavern.

Alistair motions to the lit torches stacked by the side of the door, and they each take one. 'The secret cavern of the lamp has been in my family for centuries,' he says, and adds quietly, 'My parents died keeping it secret from the ogre queen.'

Filomena puts a sympathetic hand on his shoulder. 'I'm sorry, Alistair.'

He sighs. 'I was just a baby. I don't even remember them. Anyway, there's no use feeling bad about things that happened so long ago. Come on.'

The cavern is mouldy and dark, but the deeper the group goes the lighter it gets. When they round a bend, they are bathed in luminescence.

'Wait till the dragons get a load of this,' says Filomena, scanning a room that is stacked from floor to ceiling with gold, precious gems and treasures of all kinds.

'Er, yeah, don't tell them,' says Alistair. 'Family legend says this was an ancient dragon hoard.'

Jack is running nimbly up and down the treasure pile and looking around. There are a lot of lamps. 'So where is it?'

'I'm not exactly sure,' says Alistair. 'I think it's in one of these treasure chests.'

'You don't know?' asks Filomena accusingly.

'Um, Aladdin got married a while back, OK? And I wasn't the one who put it away,' says Alistair crossly. He removes a key ring from his pocket and begins distributing the keys to the group. 'We're just going to have to open all the chests till we find it.'

Jack and Rolf begin to stack the treasure chests in a row so that Alistair, Gretel and Filomena can open them with the keys Alistair handed out. It's tedious work finding the right key for the right lock, and the treasure chests contain a variety of items.

'Tablecloths?' asks Gretel, opening one and finding folded linens inside.

'Um, Alistair?' says Filomena, finding a trove of baby pictures in another.

'One man's junk is another man's treasure,' says Alistair. 'I told you, these are family heirlooms.'

'I don't know why we worried so much about the ogres getting their hands on the lamp. If we can't find it, I doubt they can,' says Jack, mopping his head.

'Hold on!' calls Rolf from the other side of the cavern. 'I think I have something!'

They look up to see him holding a large oil lamp, made of pure gold and encrusted with dazzling diamonds.

'No, that's not it,' says Alistair. 'It was a small one. Old and rusty.'

They are crestfallen.

At last they have opened each treasure chest and spilled

the contents on to the cavern floor.

No lamp.

'It has to be here,' says Alistair. 'We just need to keep looking.'

Jack, who's been scanning the edges of the room, runs back. 'I found a second tunnel over there. I think it leads to another treasure room.'

Alistair shrugs. 'Can't hurt. Let's go.'

Chapter Forty-Two

Darkness

They are following Jack, who's using the Seeing Eye to lead them to the other cavern, when Filomena hears something. It's very faint. Water dripping? Footsteps? Or just her mind playing tricks on her in the dark?

She tries to focus on the sound, but there's nothing. She's just jumpy.

Next to her, Alistair looks glum. 'I'm the only one of my family left, the last of the Bartholomew Barnabys,' he says. 'I'm supposed to keep it safe. The lamp, I mean.'

'You've done that,' says Filomena. 'The ogres don't have it.'

'I guess. But we don't, either.'

Filomena can't argue with that. 'I hope no one stole it.'

'No one can. I'm the only one who can open the cavern,' Alistair says. Then he confesses, 'I guess I thought I'd somehow sense where the lamp is. Like, it would call to me or something.'

'Really? It does that?'

'I don't know. I thought it did,' says Alistair miserably. 'My parents didn't live long enough to tell me all their secrets. They just left the map and the camels, and that's it.'

Jack, who's walking swiftly ahead of them, suddenly stops and makes a motion for quiet. 'Did you hear that?'

Rolf sniffs the air. 'I didn't hear it, but I smelled it.'

'What is it?' asks Gretel fearfully.

They wait in silence, the darkness closes in on them, and the only light is the dim glow from Jack's Seeing Eye illuminating the fear on their faces.

'Shh,' says Rolf when Alistair starts to speak. He nods to Jack. 'We're not alone.'

Jack nods back, puts a hand on his Dragon's Tooth sheath, and turns to the rest of them. 'Get ready.'

Filomena thinks everyone can hear her heart pounding – it's thumping right out of her chest. She steadies her hand on her sword. She's faced ogres before; she can face them again. Of course the ogres have followed them all the way here. The trolls probably told them what happened and where they were headed.

But Alistair isn't paying attention. He has knelt in the darkness and is rooting around, as if he's dropped something . . . or found something. 'Guys . . . wait . . .' he says.

'Silence!' commands Rolf.

Alistair stops.

The cavern is so quiet, and at first they don't hear any sound at all . . . so quiet that it feels as if the cave itself is holding its breath.

There's nothing.

Just the sound of their breathing.

Water dripping from the roof of the cave . . .

But then . . .

There it is . . .

A wolf howl.

A warning.

Chapter Forty-Three

Cry Wolf

'HUNTERS! THEY'RE HERE!' Rolf yells, before turning into the Big Bad Wolf that he is. The rest of the pack transforms as well, snarling and leaping into the fray.

All at once, battle breaks out around them. They're surrounded by ogres on every side. The wolves howl and attack, throwing themselves against their sworn enemies, while Jack's sword clashes against ogre hammer.

Filomena kicks and stabs her way past a group of ogres swinging their mallets. Gretel screams as she wields her sword, making sure that blood doesn't get on her new dress.

But there are too many of them.

One of the ogres swings a massive arm at Jack, knocking him down.

'Jack!' Alistair yells, rushing to help his friend. He takes two steps before another ogre stomps over, blocking his path to Jack.

The ogre lets out a grunt as he swats Alistair away, sending him flying in the air until he hits the cavern wall with a thud.

Filomena turns at the sound of Alistair's groan. She wants to help him, but she's too far away. The wolves and ogres are locked in fierce battle. There are three ogres to one wolf and, as much as the wolves bite and tear, the ogres are huge and many.

'Get away from him, you monster!' Gretel screams at the ogre who has overpowered Rolf. She sinks her blade into his back, and the ogre slumps.

But the rest of the pack isn't faring as well.

They've got to get out of here.

Filomena tries to make her way to her fallen friends. But Alistair, lying on the ground, is desperately pointing to something.

What does he want?

What is he pointing at?

Then she understands.

Before Alistair was attacked, he had chanced on something. He was looking for something in the dark. No, he had *found* something.

The lamp!

She has to get to it before any of the ogres do.

She ducks down and begins to crawl while the battle rages around her. Maybe they won't notice. Maybe she'll be OK. She'll get the lamp and somehow make all this right.

She inches forward, then freezes. She turns round and sees that Alistair has been captured. He's in the clutches of a very large and very angry ogre who is screaming, spitting in his face. 'ALI BABA, WHERE IS THE LAMP?'

'I don't know!' squeaks Alistair. 'It's not here!'

'Tell us or die lying!' the ogre warns.

Alistair closes his eyes and waits for the worst.

With the ogres focused on Alistair, they don't notice Filomena. She's just a few feet away. She's almost there when Jack calls out, begging the ogres to leave Alistair alone.

'He doesn't have it! Let him go!' Jack yells.

'Is that you again, Stalker?' the ogre asks. 'Killed a giant but couldn't save your own family!'

The other ogres join in to taunt and jeer at Jack.

'And you certainly won't be able to save your friend,' the ogre says with a laugh, then turns to his companions. 'We don't need him alive, you lazy fools.'

'My pleasure,' another ogre responds with a cruel smile, moving to catch Jack.

But Jack is too quick.

Too nimble.

He jumps out of the way.

Filomena reaches the spot where Alistair was pointing. She looks around. *Where is it? Where is the lamp?*

She tries to tune out the screaming, tune out the wolves' roaring, tune out her fear for her friends. She just has to find it.

'C'mon,' Filomena mutters in frustration, frantically searching the dusty floor for the hidden treasure.

Then she sees it.

A tiny bottle with a stopper.

Aladdin's lamp.

Just an old, small, rusty oil lamp, that's all it is. Centuries old. Been in my family for generations. Stolen from a dragon's hoard.

She reaches for it, almost curling her fingers around it, just as a giant hand clasps her arm.

Chapter Forty-Four

Ogre's Wrath Indeed

'GOT YOU!' The ogre laughs.

Filomena grimaces as his laughter washes over her. The ogre is practically breathing in her face. Trapped in his grip, she can't reach for her sword. All she can do is endure the smelly and clammy assault. The stench is enough to almost make her pass out. 'Ever hear of a breath mint?' she asks.

The ogre tightens his grip and looks Filomena straight in the eye. 'Shut up about snacks before you become one,' he says menacingly.

Filomena wonders if this is the end for her. Then a

thunderbolt crashes to the ground next to her. The earth cracks, and the rumble knocks everyone off balance. The ogre drops Filomena just as another thunderbolt strikes. This one crashes into the cave wall, breaking the first layer of the surface into pieces. As the rock topples and settles on the ground, more thunderbolts strike in rapid succession, followed by the maniacal laughter that Filomena has heard before.

In the chaos, Filomena grabs the tiny lamp and stuffs it into her pocket. 'I have it! I have the lamp!' she cries. But there's no time to celebrate.

'She's here!' the ogres cheer. 'The queen!'

The queen. The legendary ogress, the one who has kept all of Never After in fear of her growing power.

'It's her!' cry the wolves, back to their boy and girl selves again.

One more flash of lighting and the ogre queen appears in the cave.

Queen Olga of Orgdale is as beautiful and as terrible as she had been on the day of the christening.

Her golden locks flying, her face as cold as winter. 'Where is it?' she hisses in a voice like snakes and sandpaper.

'Where's what?' says Jack bravely.

Olga turns to him and gasps. 'YOU!' she screeches.

'You're the little thief who killed my husband!'

Jack stands his ground without flinching. 'Your ogre husband was starving all the villages. I stole what we needed to survive, that's all. And I didn't kill him. He fell!'

'You little worm! I'll have my revenge yet! Now hand it over!' Olga screams.

'We don't have it,' says Alistair.

'LIES!' she yells as she transforms into the horrible ogre that she truly is, bulbous and oily and rotten. 'HAND ME THE LAMP!'

'Never!' yells Filomena. 'You'll never have it!'

Olga laughs again, and this time the laughter is low, throaty and intimate. 'And who in all of fairyland are you?'

In answer, the mark on Filomena's forehead shines in the darkness. 'I am under the protection of the fairy Carabosse!'

Olga laughs again. 'Oh, Carabosse, she tried her best, didn't she? Thirteenth fairy. Protective aunt. Vengeful sister. Fairy godmother. Prophecies and curses and claims to the throne. She thought she was so clever. But all the mortals believe my lies! Her story is ended! The fairies are gone. Never After is mine!' She seethes and stomps. 'NOW, ENOUGH! GIVE ME THE LAMP!'

The cavern plunges into darkness once more, and this

time when the light returns, Filomena sees that all her friends have an ogre's blade at their throats.

'Don't give it to her,' says Jack. 'You can't. Or we will be lost forever.'

'The story can't end here,' begs Alistair.

'Do what you need to do,' advises Gretel. 'Don't give that old bag anything.'

'The wolves are with you,' Rolf promises.

Filomena grips the lamp, so small and sweaty in her fist.

'Choose, mortal. Your friends or this lamp.'

In the end, Filomena remembers that she's never had friends. And so it's an easy thing to hand over.

Chapter Forty-Five

The Rules of Magic

'Your heart is bigger than your brain,' Olga sneers as she snaps up the lamp in her taloned fingers.

The ogres push the group to the centre of the cavern.

'Are you guys OK?' Filomena asks.

Jack nods.

Alistair is wild with fear. 'You gave her the lamp!'

'I had to! She was going to kill you all!'

'That's still a possibility,' says Rolf.

They watch helplessly as Olga strokes the lamp, practically cooing to it as she rubs it once, twice, three times. 'My time was stolen after Rosanna's belly was swollen. A blasted fairy came along, with a love that was strong. In my scheme she did pry, my desire denied, due to the curse that she cried. The princess is hidden, my feast my treat! Now show me the princess who's good enough to eat!'

But nothing happens.

Then a genie floats out of the lamp, looking incredibly annoyed. 'You rang?'

'Stupid thing,' the queen barks, smacking the lamp with one of her hands. 'I *said* . . . show me where Princess Eliana is hiding!'

The genie raises an eyebrow. 'I am the genie of the lamp. My power is vast and uncontrollable. Once you make a wish, it's non-negotiable.'

Olga glares at the genie. 'SHOW ME THE PRINCESS!' she yells.

The genie shakes his head in a way that indicates Olga has no manners.

'WHERE IS ELIANA?' she demands.

In answer, the genie motions to the lamp.

Olga looks down at the lamp. There is a mark on it now. A mark that glows in the darkness.

A mark that looks all too familiar.

Wait a minute . . .

Filomena knows that symbol. It's the same one that marks her forehead, and she reaches out to touch it.

Olga looks at the symbol on Filomena's forehead. 'You!'

Filomena is paralysed. *Me?*

The princess has been missing for thousands of years. But time is different in the mortal world and Never After. Mere days in the mortal world are centuries in this world.

Some say the princess was hidden. Some say the princess was eaten.

But the princess is here. *She* is the princess.

The ogre queen is drooling, ready to cut her into pieces and feast on her flesh. There's no escaping now. Somehow she's always known she'd be ogre toast.

'Filomena!' It's Jack, startling her into action. 'Make a wish!' he yells. And Filomena realizes that when Olga smacked the lamp away, it rolled near her foot.

'Go on,' says the genie, looking bored. 'I haven't got all day.'

Filomena picks up the lamp and quickly rubs it three times. 'GENIE OF THE LAMP, GET RID OF OLGA OF ORGDALE!'

The genie sighs. 'As you wish.'

Prologue

The UnWritten

When Carabosse wakes up, she is in a different world. It's a world both strange and fascinating. The people of this world think that she and the rest of her kin are mere figments of their imagination. She has her niece in a basket. But she can't keep her. She doesn't know enough about this world to keep her safe. And so she looks for those who will. She finds them in a tidy house with a neat garden. They write books, she soon discovers. Good. They will believe in things they cannot see. Perhaps they will believe this.

She kisses her baby niece for the last time and marks

the baby with her power, her memories and part of her soul. Then she hides the mark.

Next she pins a note to the baby's blanket and leaves her underneath the protection of an oak tree.

She watches them read the note, and cry, and pick up the baby.

> *To the Lord and Lady Jefferson-Cho,*
> *The kind couple of 101 Creekside Lane,*
>
> *You have longed for a child for so many years.*
> *Take this babe with my blessing.*
> *Keep her safe, for there are those who will harm her.*
> *Witches and ogres, giants and trolls will come looking.*
> *You must remain vigilant. Protect and defend her.*
> *Hide her away if you can.*
> *I have faith in you both.*
> *I remain forever in your debt.*
> *Her name is*

'What does that say? I can't read that part,' says the mother Bettina is her name.

'Her name is Ilomena? No, wait, I think it says Renia?

Or . . . Elvira?' says the dad, who is called Carter.

Bettina makes a face. 'Not Elvira.'

The dad looks at the letter closely. 'Filomena?'

'Filomena, that's pretty,' says the mum.

'Filomena,' repeats the dad, and smiles.

'Filomena Jefferson-Cho,' says the mum proudly. 'That's who she is.'

'Whoever wrote this was crying,' says the dad. 'That inkblot is from a tear. I know it is.'

Carabosse wipes her face and leaves them. She has more to do before time runs out. She decides she will write the stories of her world. She will write them true. She writes and writes and writes, and she leaves the books at the office of a well-known publisher. Perhaps the stories will spread far and wide. She chooses a name for herself and leaves a photograph of herself, a little bit of magic captured in the frame. She dedicates each book to one of her sisters.

But now her magic is fading. It has taken everything and more to cast the spell, to bring her niece to safety, to write the books. She will not live to see it finished. That is Eliana's task now. The fairy's gossamer gown begins to fade, and soon Carabosse does too, until all that is left of her is the mark on a baby girl's forehead.

Chapter Forty-Six

Victory

Filomena wished to get rid of the witch of Orgdale. Except nothing happens. The genie smiles mysteriously. 'Child of the Forest and the Castle, niece of Carabosse and daughter of Rosanna, you have everything in your power to see your wish come true. I will leave you with that.' The genie disappears.

'A whole lot of help he is,' grumbles Alistair.

'Genies. I told you they're unpredictable,' says Jack.

'Hang on, *you're* Princess Eliana?' asks Alistair, pointing to Filomena. 'The cursed baby?'

'Yeah, that's me. Weird, huh?' says Filomena.

'Not really,' says Alistair.

'WATCH OUT!' yells Jack, and Filomena turns to see Olga throwing the lamp at her in rage.

'YOU WON'T GET RID OF ME THAT EASILY!' the ogre queen yells.

Jack dives in front of Filomena like a football player, arms reaching for the lamp as he does so. With his quick action, he manages to stop the lamp from connecting with Filomena's face and prevents it from hitting the ground, where it likely would have smashed into pieces. He hits the ground instead, with a loud thud, and rapidly slides across the cavern floor. Rolling, with the lamp intact, he hugs it in his arms to shield it from damage on the hard ground.

He holds it up. 'Alistair! Catch!'

Alistair is ready.

The lamp flies across the cavern, and this time he catches it and puts it in his pocket.

Olga launches herself at Filomena in fury, but the wolves are ready too. Rolf and his pack have transformed back into beasts. They attack the ogres, and Olga and her soldiers have no recourse but to retreat.

'Don't give up, you fools!' Olga screams.

But the ogres are cowards, and they run from the

wolves and the children with the sharp blades.

At last Olga turns away as well, slithering and disappearing into the shadows.

'Get her!' Filomena cries, pointing at the queen's shadow now quickly slinking from sight.

The wolves give chase, taking after her without hesitation. They run on all fours, disappearing in a furry frenzy while Jack, Alistair, Gretel and Filomena follow, swords drawn in the air.

'Hey, Fil!' says Alistair.

'What?'

'This time we're running after them! We're not running away!'

'It's another reason to run!' Filomena laughs.

They weave through the cavern's paths, turning and twisting with each route they take. The light is faint, but the further they go the easier it becomes to see, the way out becoming closer and closer with each step.

Once they reach the outside of the cave, the hot sun beats down on them. The open expanse of the dry desert looms before them, and the ogres are just barely in sight.

Olga turns round. 'ENOUGH! I will not be disgraced and chased by a group of children and dogs! You may have your wretched kingdom! We will go back to Orgdale, but we shall return!'

With that last threat, ogress queen and her soldiers disappear in a cloud of black smoke.

The wolves turn back into boys and girls. Gretel picks sand out of her hair. Jack cleans his sword, and Alistair holds on to the lamp.

He holds it up to the light. 'Huh.' Alistair tosses the lamp to the sand.

'What are you doing?' asks Filomena.

'It's over. The genie's gone. That must have been his last wish,' Alistair explains. 'He's free.'

'Genies are nuisances, anyway,' says Jack.

'So . . . you're a princess. Doesn't that mean you have to marry a prince?' says Alistair, making googly eyes.

Filomena frowns. 'I'm not marrying some dumb prince. That might have been my destiny once. But it's not any more. It's just like it says in the books. We gotta write our own stories.'

Jack turns away, so they can't see his face, but Filomena thinks he is smiling.

Chapter Forty-Seven

More Adventures Await

Filomena's back home in North Pasadena, where nothing ever happens. The sun is shining. The birds are chirping. The weather is warm and ordinary. Since her return home, the most exciting thing that's happened was when she spilled a plate of hot spaghetti all over her white T-shirt.

Her parents told her everything, andshowed her theletter and the basket.

In Westphalia, the thorns disappeared. The kingdom awoke. And they discovered that King Vladimir had been killed, his corpse rotting in the middle of the ballroom, where he had tried to kill Olga and save his daughter. Her father died fighting for her. She will never know him, but she knows she was loved.

Filomena knows who she is now. She is the daughter of Vladimir and Rosanna, and she has a whole family in Never After. Zera told her she can come visit any time.

But she also knows who she *really* is. She might be Princess Eliana of Westphalia, but she will always be Filomena Jefferson-Cho of North Pasadena, California, and her parents are Bettina Jefferson and Carter Cho. She is their kin. For love is thicker than blood. And she has been theirs since the moment they found her in their yard.

She tells her parents this.

They are glad. But they also tell her that she's grounded.

Especially when they hear she was back in Hollywood and did not call them. But it's not like she was ever allowed out much in the first place. So, in reality, being grounded felt no different from any other day. She's stayed mostly in her room, reading, doing homework and other non-adventurous things of that nature.

It was hard to say goodbye to her friends in Never After. *Her friends.* How about that. So many. Even snarky Sid.

Gretel wanted to come back too. She decided she'd be

biportal and go between the fairy and mortal worlds. They promised to hang sometime.

Luckily, before she left the Never After, Filomena asked Zera for a favour. An enchantment or spell to hide the mark of the thirteenth fairy. Her aunt explained that she couldn't make it disappear forever, but she could conceal it. Now, if Filomena ever wants to see it, all she has to do is shine a flashlight on the spot on her skin and utter these words: *Carabosse, Carabosse, if you're near, present the mark of the thirteenth fairy and make it clear.*

So now, with that mark no longer visible on her forehead, she doesn't have to wear beanies to school and pretend she has lice. *It's the little things*, she reminds herself. And since she lost her backpack in Never After (*her parents sure weren't thrilled when she told them she left it there*), they brought her brand-new copies of the books she'd left behind. Matter of fact, they bought her the entire series. Only this version has updated covers! Jack has a few more companions – a dark, curly-haired princess, a stylish fashion designer and an entire wolf pack, in addition to the loyal Alistair.

As she sits on her bed, with her little fluffy Pomeranian, Adelina Jefferson-Cho, nuzzling against her leg, Filomena flips open one of the books. Right where she'd left off reading last night. Being grounded isn't bad at all, in her opinion. It's basically the same thing as not being grounded. And, in her case, apparently you get rewards, like a new backpack and new books.

'Filomena!' her mother calls from downstairs. 'Come down, honey! It's time for dinner!'

'Coming, Mum!' Filomena yells back, putting her book down open-faced on her bed to save her spot. She never has a bookmark when she needs one.

She puts on her slippers and calls Adelina to follow her, then heads down the steps with a skip to join her parents in the kitchen. The familiar bag of delivery dinner sits on the counter, and the aroma of lemon and chicken sifts through the room.

'Mmm,' Filomena hums. 'Is that what I think it is?' She eyes the bag hungrily, rubbing her hands together as she takes her seat at the table.

'Yup,' her father responds with a grin. 'Only *the* best chicken francese from your favourite restaurant.'

Filomena does a little dance in her seat, making her father chuckle. 'I should get in trouble more often.'

This earns her a warning glare from her mother, who says, 'I don't think so. And, hey, up.' She beckons Filomena with her pointer finger. 'Come and help me set the table.' She sets down three plates and three bowls on the counter.

Filomena gets up, carries the dishes to the table, and sets them down in their appropriate places. Then she grabs three napkins and folds them in triangles, placing them next to each plate.

While her mother is rummaging through the silverware drawer for forks and knives, there's a knock at the front door.

Filomena and her parents exchange curious glances, and her father says, 'I wonder who that could be. Are you expecting anyone, honey?' he asks his wife.

'No . . .' she says, almost as if asking a question. 'Fil? Are you?'

Filomena shakes her head, confused. 'No. Come on. You guys know I don't have any friends.' The Fettucine Alfredos have disappeared from school – the only explanation was that they had transferred – but Maggie Martin found another group to hang out with.

'I'll go see who it is,' she says, half hoping for something, though she's not quite sure what.

She peeps through the hole to see who it is, and smiles. For just outside, on her doorstep, are Jack, Gretel and Alistair.

Filomena opens the door. There they are. Gretel, her hair in a high ponytail; Alistair, looking no worse for wear after being squeezed by ogres; and Jack, his vines popping out of his arms, that jaunty green cap on his forehead.

'Hey,' says Jack.

'Hey,' says Filomena.

'You look fabulous!' says Gretel. 'Is that your school uniform? So chic.'

'You guys should come in. We're having dinner. Mum and Dad will insist you join us,' Filomena tells them.

'Oooooh,' says Alistair.

'No time,' says Jack. 'We're not just dropping by to say hi. This is important.'

'What's going on?'

Jack lowers his voice. 'The Stolen Slipper. We've got to get it back.'

'For Cinderella?' Filomena asks, confused.

'*From* Cinderella,' says Gretel. 'That wench!'

Filomena scrunches her face in response. If she remembers the story correctly . . .

Oh, never mind, she thinks as she recalls previous versions of stories that are blatantly untrue or false, at least according to the people who actually *live* in fairy tales.

Filomena is about to cross the doorstep when she stops.

'Wait, I forgot something!' She rushes back inside, closes the door and heads to her bedroom, where she grabs a book.

'I started writing the thirteenth book,' Filomena informs them, out of breath from running upstairs and back down so fast. 'But not all the pages are filled in.'

'So let's fill them in,' says Jack.

'You *are* coming, aren't you?' Gretel asks. 'I blew off a nail appointment for this. You'd *better* come!'

Alistair stifles a laugh and Jack elbows him, letting him know it's time to be serious.

Filomena looks back and forth among her small group of Never After pals, each of them awaiting her response with eager and expectant eyes. In that moment, she realizes she just accidentally lied to her parents . . . again.

'Mum, Dad, come over and meet my friends. Because I *do* have friends,' she says. 'They're just not from school.'

Her parents come over to meet everyone, and there's a lot of hugging and handshakes.

'You've got to go back to Never After, don't you?' asks Mum.

Filomena nods.

'Be brave,' says Dad. 'And come home to us.'

'Group hug!' she says, holding on to both of her parents as tightly as she can.

They let go. They let her go.

Now she and her friends are on to their next adventure. But not before they hunt down a couple of cheeseburgers.

Acknowledgements

As always, a book is a journey an author does not take alone. So many thanks to my longtime dearest friends in publishing and out: my editor Jennifer Besser and my agent Richard Abate. I am so lucky to have you in my life and my books! Thank you to everyone at Macmillan, 3Arts and Gotham Group, especially Martha Stevens, Brittany Pearlman and Ellen Goldsmith-Vein. Shout out to my friends who love books as much as I do: Margie Stohl, Raf Simon and Jill Stewart. My husband Mike Johnston writes books too, and has been a huge part of mine, and is always there for the cackling and the kvetching. Both my parents were huge readers who always bought me any book I ever wanted from the bookstore. Every book I write is for my daughter Mattea. Thank you to my readers!

About the Author

Melissa de la Cruz is the *New York Times* number one bestselling author of many critically acclaimed and award-winning novels for readers of all ages. Her novel *The Isle of the Lost*, the prequel to the Disney Channel movie, *The Descendants*, spent fifteen weeks on the *NYT* bestseller list at number one and has over one million copies in print. She has written two sequels and a novel for Marvel. Melissa grew up in Manila and now lives in Hollywood, USA.